Life Here On Earth

by
Nila D. Bond

Edited by Marie Todd.
Cover photography by Darla DeLome.
Graphic design and illustrations by Mallory Wilson.

*For my sisters, Kitty, Jenny, and Glenda…also known
respectively as Gammy, GiGi, and Meme
and
for all those who readily take on the role of a
grandmother figure.*

Chapter 1

1973 Southeast Texas

The sun just began peeking over the tall pines in the back yard as Verleen took her last sip of coffee. She sat on the back porch of the small farm house as the night gave way to the early morning's faint glow that grew to chase the darkness away. *Guess I'd better get to movin'. The chickens won't feed themselves.* As she took one more look at the woods that surrounded her home, she sighed with satisfaction. *Even though I've never been one much for travelin', I don't think there's a prettier place on this earth than right here.*

As she got up from the wooden rocker, she felt the stiffness in her joints that had been her companion for the last few years. Taking a few steps to the edge of the porch, she tossed the last dregs of coffee from her cup. Just then, Boone left his sleeping position beside the chair and came to stand next to her. His ears were standing straight up and he was staring at the edge of the yard where the thick pine forest began. "What is it, boy? Did you spot a deer?" It was pretty commonplace for deer to wander into her yard and graze on the lawn.

In answer, the mutt began baying and prancing in place. He looked up at her and then back to the woods. He shot off the porch and came to a halt at the edge of the trees. As he stared into the woods in silence, he trembled all over and the hair stood up on his back.

"Boone, what's gotten into you? What's out there?"

The dog did not seem to hear her. It was locked onto something that had him spooked. After a few moments, he took off at a dead run into the forest and Verleen could hear him crashing through the underbrush.

"Boone, get back here!...That dog has never minded me. Don't know why I even feed the old thang and keep him around," she grumbled. But she did know why. Ever since Boone had appeared six years ago on her back porch, hungry and half starved, he had adopted her and was always underfoot. Given that she had been living alone in the farmhouse for many years, it was comforting to have another soul around to talk to even if the old fleabag couldn't hold up his end of the conversation.

Verleen slipped into the house to grab a denim jacket to slip over her work shirt and trousers before starting the morning chores. There was always a lot to do on her small farm and it was messy work that would ruin nice outfits. *Can't remember the last time I bothered putting on a dress. Was it Gracie's daughter's wedding? Maybe someone's funeral?* Farming and fancy clothes just didn't go together. Besides the chickens to be fed, there was her cow, Bessie, that had to be milked every day. The frost on the ground crunched underfoot as she headed across the yard to the barn. It was most likely the last cool snap before spring arrived and Verleen was glad. *These nights when the temps dip down are hard on my old bones. Guess that's just part of makin' it to the age of 75. The secret is to keep movin' and keep workin' 'til God calls me home. If he's allowin' me to see another day, then my work here is not yet done.*

While Verleen might have been considered elderly by some standards, she did not move or carry herself in an aged manner and generally exhibited a lot of spirit and spunk. The farm chores kept her physically active and she was able to stay on top of the upkeep that the place required.

The morning passed quickly as she fed and watered all the animals and milked Bessie. As she crossed the yard toward the house with the pail of fresh milk, she stopped by the part of the yard that would soon become the vegetable garden and spent a few minutes mentally planning where the neat rows would go. Her garden always produced a plentiful amount of vegetables each year that she enjoyed at her table. She shared the produce with her neighbors and friends and still had plenty to can for the winter. Not that winters were overly harsh and demanding in this part of the country. The temperatures only dipped down into freezing once or twice during the winter months and it rarely stayed that cold for very long. Verleen had only seen it snow in Southeast Texas once or twice in her lifetime, and it had been a light dusting of white powder that quickly melted as soon as the sun had come up.

Once the outside work was done, she entered the house by the back door leaving her rubber boots out on the porch and tackled her kitchen chores in her bare feet. She kept her floors spotless and liked the feel of the worn linoleum on her soles. She only wore slippers around the house on the coldest of days. *You can take the girl out of the country, but you can't take the country out of the girl, I reckon.* She took the pail of fresh milk from the breakfast table and began pouring it into gallon jars, straining it through a cheesecloth filter, and setting it into the refrigerator to cool.

Old John will be 'round soon. I'd better get lunch started. Verleen browned some stew meat on the stove and added canned vegetables from her pantry. The herbs and spices that went into the pot created a wonderful aroma as it simmered and bubbled on the back burner. She was just pulling a cast-iron skillet of browned cornbread out of the oven when she heard steps on the back porch.

"Come on in, Mistah John. You have perfect timing as usual. How did you know that I was just settin' the table?" she hollered through the screen door.

The door hinges creaked as he stepped into the kitchen and Old John just smiled slightly and dipped his head as he removed his black felt hat. As was his custom, he stood in the doorway as if unsure of his welcome.

"Sit down. It's all ready," Verleen said.

Old John took his usual place and she set a bowl of steaming soup in front of him with a side plate of hot cornbread. Old John sat quietly waiting for Verleen to sit down also. After she said a few short words of grace, they both picked up their spoons and dug in. Little was said as they ate in comfortable silence. They had been friends for several years now and words were not necessary between them. Verleen went to the stove and cut another piece of cornbread bringing it back to the table for Old John. He glanced up and nodded appreciatively when she set it down by his bowl. Later over coffee and cake, Verleen's remarks about the weather and the progress of her garden only elicited small sounds of agreement and head nods from Old John for he was a man of few words...very few words.

No one knew much about Old John, what his last name was or where he came from. He never talked about himself or much of anything for that matter. He lived alone in an old shack by a creek that ran through the woods. Verleen supposed that he was a recluse and she couldn't really blame him for keeping to his own company. *I'm sure he's seen enough meanness in his lifetime that he can do without the fellowship of the people hereabouts.* His charcoal skin was wrinkled and what hair remained on his head was gray, wiry, and cut close to his scalp. He seemed ancient and ageless at the same time.

Old John appeared out of the forest one day as Verleen attempted to chop up a small tree that had fallen in her yard. Without a word, he began stacking wood by the house and took over the chopping when she had set the axe down. After they cleaned up the debris, they sat in the rockers on the porch drinking ice tea and eating sandwiches. From then on, when Verleen returned from her errands in town, she found random improvements had occurred on the farm. The hole in the chicken pen fence would be magically fixed. She discovered firewood split and stacked and the rickety front step replaced. It was as if little elves had emerged from the forest, gone to work, and then disappeared as quickly as they had come.

Verleen started watching for her new friend and managed to catch him slipping into her back yard one day. She hollered out the window for him to come in for lunch just as if he had been expected, and he came to the back door apprehensively. Opening the screen door and waving him in and to the table, they began an unlikely friendship that continued to this day. Keeping his eyes on his plate that day, he informed her that everyone called him Old John and that was the most information she had ever gotten from him. Not being one to pester a body, Verleen figured that she knew all she needed. Over the years, he continued to do repairs around her place and showed up for meals a few times a week. If she left the farm for a day or two, she always made sure that she left the back door unlatched and that there was food in the refrigerator for him. She knew when he had been by because any dishes used were found washed and in the drain board. It was a friendly arrangement that suited both of them.

The old gentleman pushed back his chair and stood up. "Mighty fine meal, Miz Vee. I sure thank you," he said in his raspy, quiet voice. From the beginning she tried to get him to call her Verleen but he ignored her request and always called her Miz Vee.

"Don't forget your food on the counter." She always cooked enough so that she could send him home with extra food. He detoured by the counter and picked up the brown paper sack holding mason jars of soup with cornbread and cake wrapped in foil. He donned his hat as he shuffled out the door, and she watched from the window over the sink as he crossed the yard and disappeared down a path that meandered through the tall trees into the pine forest.

She spent the next half hour clearing the table and washing up the dishes. Hanging her apron on a wall hook, she went out the back door to settle in a rocker as the day was warming nicely having already melted the light frost in the yard. Boone had apparently not returned from his jaunt into the woods but Verleen was not worried. He often left the porch to explore the surrounding area. He was even known to stay gone a day or two only to return later starving and exhausted.

A cool breeze played with the loose gray tendrils of hair around her face. The slow rocking motion of her chair and the birds singing in the yard brought about a sense of peace and calm and she felt herself being lulled into a light slumber. Resting her head against the back of her chair, she gave into the languid state that was stealing over her whole body and soon she was snoring lightly.

Sometime later she felt someone nudge her knee…someone with a cold, wet nose. Opening one eye, she peered down and saw Boone sitting at her feet. "There you are, you old rascal. Where you been?" she mumbled softly and began to close her eyes once more. Boone wasn't having it. He nudged her knee again and this time licked her lax hand lying in her lap. "I'm trying to nap, you pest. Go find yourself a nice, warm spot in the sunshine and have a rest," she said sternly without opening her eyes.

This time Boone leaned his entire weight against her legs and whined to get her attention. Verleen yawned and grudgingly opened her eyes to look down at the mutt. "Okay, what is it, old boy?" Seeing that she was now awake, Boone scampered to the top of the steps and looked back at her. Mystified by his uncharacteristic behavior, she watched him for a few minutes. He pranced excitedly in place and wagged his tail. *Did I forget to fill his food bowl this mornin'?* A glance about the porch showed not only was his food bowl half full but so was his water container. She got up from her chair and stretched her stiff limbs. Seeing her standing prompted Boone to bound down the steps and into the yard a few feet. He halted and looked back at her as if to say, "Come on…I'm waitin'." Verleen paused briefly and then decided to follow. "You sure are acting strangely today. What's gotten into you?"

As she got closer to Boone, he sprinted a few more feet across the yard and looked back, impatiently waiting for her to catch up. A few moments later, they reached the farthest edge of the mowed area where the thick trees took over. Boone stood stock still staring into the undergrowth. Verleen halted beside him and scanned the surrounding area. "Alright, you brought me out here, Boone. What's goin' on?"

Boone, of course, did not answer, so seeing nothing of interest, she sighed and shook her head. The rocker was calling her back to finish the nap that had been so rudely interrupted. Just as she started to turn away and head to the porch, her eyes landed on something in the weeds…something that she had almost missed and it caused her breath to catch. She froze in place beside the mutt and gawked in surprise.

Chapter 2

Verleen had seen many a wild creature in her forest: snakes, opossums, raccoons, hoot owls, squirrels and the like, but she had never seen anything like this before. Crouched in the thick grass staring back at her was the skinniest, dirtiest little boy on God's green earth. He wore the look of a spooked, wild creature, ready to run off if she made any quick movements.

She purposefully made her voice soft and non-threatening. "You sure look hungry, little feller. How 'bout I get you something to eat? Stay put and I'll be right back." She slowly backed away and turned to casually stroll up to the house. Looking over her shoulder, she saw that Boone had not moved a muscle. She hastily assembled a sandwich and dropped some cookies beside it on the plate. Careful not to slam the back door, she returned to the edge of the yard. The boy still cowered there in the tall grass and had yet to make a sound. She set the plate and a glass of milk on the ground beside Boone, grasped the dog by the collar, and both returned to sit on the wooden steps of the porch.

It was several long minutes before the boy emerged from the weeds to cautiously squat by the plate. Keeping his eyes suspiciously on Verleen and Boone, he began to wolf down the sandwich and chug the milk. *Guess hunger won out over fear. Wonder how long it's been since the little guy has had a proper meal?* That thought was quickly followed by more pressing ones. *What in the world is he doing out here all by himself? He can't be more than four years old. Where are his parents?* The little boy now gobbled the cookies, and they were disappearing so fast Verleen feared he was going to choke. "Stay, Boone," she said softly to the dog. Slipping into the house, she grabbed several more cookies and another glass of milk. While the boy watched her warily, she crossed half the distance from the steps to where he sat and placed the glass and napkin of cookies on the grass. She retreated to the steps to once again sit beside the dog.

The boy finished everything on his plate and then gaped back at the two on the steps with the biggest brown eyes that Verleen had ever seen on a child. Cookie crumbs and a milk mustache clung to the edges of his mouth and added to the filth already coating his thin face. His eyes broke away from Verleen to glance longingly at the napkin on the ground. "Go ahead, sweetheart. Those are for you. If you would like more, you can have all you want." She worked hard to keep her voice casual and friendly. *I'll never be able to catch him if he decides to run. These old legs of mine won't be able to keep up.*

The boy moved carefully toward the napkin and began to eat his second helping of cookies, albeit not quite as rapidly this time. As he chewed the last cookie, his eyes began to droop sleepily. *I think the poor child is plum wore out.* The sunshine beaming down on the verdant lawn did its part in soothing the young boy into a relaxed state. He slowly lay over onto his side with the last of the uneaten cookie still in his hand, and his eyes closed as he gave in to much-needed sleep.

Verleen sat perfectly still for 15 minutes to give deep slumber a chance to take over and then she rose from the steps. Walking silently over to the boy, she gently scooped him up and headed for the house. *He weighs no more than a sack of feathers!* Depositing him on the living room couch, she tucked a pillow under his head and then sat in a nearby chair gazing at him. She knew most of the families and kids for several miles around, and he certainly didn't belong to any of them. He wore only a plain, torn T-shirt and a pair of jeans. The clothes were so filthy and ragged it was hard to tell what color they had originally been. "I guess when you get your nap out, you'll tell me who you are," she said as much to herself as to the small child who was lost in deep sleep.

The child continued to sleep without stirring for the next two hours as Verleen quietly went about her housework. She was just sitting down at the kitchen table with a bowl of leftover soup when she felt a prickling on the back of her neck. "I thought you might be waking up soon," she remarked without looking around. "Come sit at the table and I'll fix you a bowl of soup."

She calmly headed for the stove and began to fill a dish for the boy. When she turned and headed back to the table, she saw that he was peeking around the doorframe that separated the small living room and kitchen. He had yet to utter a sound so she continued on as if his presence in her home was not the bizarre occurrence that it so obviously was. As she sat back down in her chair, she placed a wedge of warm cornbread beside his bowl and then slathered the top of it with homemade butter. From the corner of her eye, she saw he looked longingly at the food even though he had yet to move a muscle.

Taking up her spoon, she slurped her soup in a rather unladylike fashion and shook her head slightly. "Mmmmm hmmmm…there ain't nothing better than hot soup and buttered cornbread when you're really hungry. I think I outdid myself this time. Cornbread's all brown and crusty on the outside but sweet and soft in the middle. Just the way I like it." She kept her attention on her food but could sense him drawing slightly closer. "Yours is getting cold, little man. If you don't like soup, I guess I can give it to Boone after while."

Verleen continued to consume her meal with gusto and eventually, the small child slid into the chair across the table. She kept up a pleasant prattle about inconsequential things as the boy set about consuming the food but did not lift his eyes to meet hers. When he had emptied his glass, she kept her movements slow and calm as she refilled it from the pitcher of iced tea. He was so small that his chin barely cleared the edge of the table, but he managed to stuff his mouth with the warm food and even polished off a thick hunk of cake before he sat back and looked directly at Verleen.

"Well, now…I feel better. How 'bout you? I was getting mighty hungry," she said with a soft smile. The boy did not respond. He just sat as if waiting to see what would happen next.

"My name is Miz Verleen Jackson. My friends call me Verleen but all the kids 'round here call me Nana Vee." She paused and then shrugged her shoulders slightly as she explained. "One of young'uns here 'bouts called me that years ago and it just sort of stuck."

They both sat still regarding each other across the table. She finally broke the silence by asking softly, "Want to tell me your name and where you came from?"

The boy sat blinking and gave no answer. "Well, I'm sure glad you found me, little man. A person can be lost for days in the Big Thicket. You're gonna be just fine. I'm gonna see to that. First thing we're gonna do is get you a nice, hot bath and find you some clean clothes."

Rising from the table she walked down the short hall to the bathroom and went in leaving the door open. She put the stopper in the claw-foot tub and turned on the taps. Hot, steamy water combined with the bubble bath soap she added and foamy suds began to gather and rise in the tub.

The little boy peered around the door and she gestured him inside. "Come on, little man. Don't be shy. My great-nieces and nephews love taking bubble baths in Nana Vee's big tub. Drop them clothes and jump in while I put supper in the fridge." Verleen headed for the kitchen, giving the boy some time to make up his mind about the bath. A few minutes later, she could hear water splashing and smiled to herself. *Never knew a kid who could resist a big, old tub of bubbles.*

Sticking her head around the open bathroom door, she remarked "My, you are a skinny little thang. Don't you worry, though. Nana Vee's gonna have you fattened up in no time. You just splash around for a bit. I'm gonna finish up in here and I'll be back directly." The boy did not reply or acknowledge her in any way. He just kept splashing and playing in the suds.

While she cleared the table of supper dishes and cleaned the kitchen, her mind kept going over all the possible scenarios of how this young boy came to be alone in the woods. *That poor child has been out there for days from the looks of him. There's nothing out there in The Big Thicket but thousands of acres of trees and some baygalls. Maybe he got separated from his folks while they was out hunting.*

Standing in the door of the bathroom, she chuckled at the sight of the little feller almost hidden by the froth. His splashing had produced a tub full of airy bubbles and several puddles on the floor. "You have managed to soak off that top layer of dirt. Let's tackle the rest." Using a washcloth, she scrubbed him all over and surprisingly he allowed it. When he was free of the grime and dirt, she pulled the plug and wrapped him in a big, fluffy towel and carried him to her bedroom and set him on the bed. "I think you've grown smaller. Looks like you were mostly made up of dirt and half of you just went down the drain," she joked. Her attempt at humor was met with a solemn look.

Rummaging through the dresser, she finally located an old, white T-shirt that was worn but clean. "This was Elmer's and it's much too big but it will do for tonight anyway. We can't have you sleeping in your birthday suit. Tomorrow I'll find you something to wear 'til we get your clothes washed." She toweled the child dry and slipped the large T-shirt over his head using a safety pin to make the neck opening smaller. His now-clean brown locks began to curl as they dried and formed a halo around his small face. "Mmmmmm mmmmm…you smell so much better now…like the sweet end of a skunk…like a butterfly's butt when he's been sittin' on a flower….like a…well, you definitely smell better than old Boone." Was it her imagination or did she see the tiniest bit of a smile threaten his somber face? Whatever it was, it was quickly gone.

Taking the boy by the hand, she led him to the small bedroom across the hall from hers. She turned on the light to reveal a bed neatly made and covered with a homemade quilt. She pulled back the covers and gestured, "Climb in, little buddy. This will be your bed and your room while you're here." The little boy gripped her hand and looked up quizzically as if asking, "I'm sleeping here?"

"Well, you didn't think I was gonna have you sleep out on the porch with the dog, did you?"

Once again, the boy had no reply but climbed up onto the bed and under the covers that Verleen had pulled back. She clicked on a small night light that sat on the bedside table and tucked the covers around the boy. Although winter was probably over in this part of the country, it wasn't quite spring yet and the evening air would grow cool as the night wore on. At the door, she paused and turned back. "I'll be right across the hall if you need me..." Her words trailed off because her unexpected, little guest was already fast asleep.

Chapter 3

Verleen peeked in on the little boy several times during the night but he slept soundly and undisturbed. She slipped quietly from her bed checking on him one more time before leaving out the back door to start the day's chores. When she returned to the house, she quickly took care of the fresh milk from Bessie, swept the floors, wiped the counters, and filled Boone's bowl on the porch. A rustle of covers had her checking once again on the boy, and she found him sitting on the side of the bed silently gazing about the small room.

"Good mornin'. Are you hungry?" she asked quietly.

As usual, his only response was to return her steady gaze with his big, brown eyes.

"I'll have breakfast ready in a few minutes," she said heading back down the hall to the kitchen.

Verleen quickly stirred up the batter for buttermilk biscuits and patted them out on a floured plate. Cutting them out in round circles with a drinking glass, she put them in a greased pan and slipped them into the oven. A few moments later, she had bacon sizzling in the skillet and was beating eggs in a bowl with a fork. Without looking around, she knew her little house guest was watching her from the kitchen doorway.

"Take a seat at the table. I fixed your chair so you could reach your plate a little bit easier from now on."

The little boy crossed the kitchen to the small dining table and looked at the cooking pot that she had upturned in the wooden chair and had covered with a cup towel. When she set a cup of orange juice in front of him, he was perched on the pot and she eyed the sitting arrangement critically and nodded with satisfaction.

"Yep, I think that's gonna work. Drink your juice and I'll have it all ready in a jiffy."

A short time later, she placed a bowl of scrambled eggs on the table followed by crispy bacon and the hot, fluffy biscuits. She heaped his plate full of food and set it in front of him. Buttering his biscuit and spooning jelly into its center, she asked, "Ever had mayhaw jelly? Folks around here just love the stuff. I sell it from the back of my truck out on the highway along with some of my garden vegetables. Some of them city folks that come through ain't never had it before, but once they try it, they always come back for more."

The boy just sat staring at her blinking owlishly.

"Go ahead, honey. Nobody goes hungry 'round Nana Vee's house," she gently prompted.

He took up his fork and dug into the hot, steaming fare and began to eat with enthusiasm.

I do love to watch a little one enjoy good food. I don't think anyone's been feeding him regular meals even before he got lost. Verleen sipped her coffee and nibbled a biscuit, taking pleasure in watching him put away seconds of everything along with a large glass of milk.

Once finished, he climbed down from his chair and she grabbed a clean, wet cloth. "Hang on…let's get that sticky jelly off your face and hands." He paused obediently and held up his hands. She carefully wiped away all traces of his breakfast remarking, "If I don't clean the sticky off you, Boone will for sure. He'll just follow you around for hours licking your face like you're an all day sucker…wait a minute, what's this?" With a look of exaggerated surprise on her face, Verleen gently poked his belly in several places. "I think I feel a biscuit right here and here's a bit of bacon. That there's a couple of eggs. Here's another biscuit…this one has jelly."

A look of wonder came over his features and he rubbed his belly and then looked up into her smiling face. A small grin put in an appearance and then a giggle escaped…and then another until he was giggling with all his might. His little face had completely transformed from his usual serious expression to one of total delight and he looked like a completely different child. Verleen's heart did a flip-flop and she felt as though her world shifted somehow. *I don't think you've laughed in so long that you'd just about forgotten how. One so young shouldn't look as though he's carrying the weight of the world.* She gazed in wonder at the boy's innocent features until his giggles subsided.

"I'll make you a deal, sweetheart. You clear the table for me and then you can go out on the porch and see what ole Boone is up to."

The little boy began cheerfully bringing the dishes to the kitchen counter and once done, he stood looking up at her expectantly. "Go on but don't leave the yard. Now that you're found, we don't want you lost again," she shooed him toward the back door.

With her hands in the hot, soapy water, Verleen watched out the window where she had a good view of the porch. As the morning sun beamed through the tall trees, it lit up the dog and the boy. Still dressed in the long T-shirt, the boy sat beside the dog on the steps and they both turned their faces up to the warmth of the sun. Boone leaned against the boy and the boy slipped his arm around the dog in a gesture of companionship.

God sent you to me for a reason, little man. I'm not sure why so we'll just have to wait and see…but rest assured, I'm gonna take real good care of you now. Verleen nodded to herself as if making up her mind, but in reality, she knew there had never really been anything to decide.

Having set the kitchen in order, she picked up the phone where it hung on the kitchen wall. She dialed a number that she knew by heart and listened to it ring.

"Hello?"

"Gracie? It's me, Verleen. You want to come over for coffee this mornin'?"

"Sure, what's up?"

"Well, I just find myself with a slow day and thought this would be a good time for us to visit."

"Okay…" Gracie said slowly. "Everything alright? You don't sound like yourself."

"Oh, the coyotes were barking and howling in the woods last night. Guess I didn't sleep too well."

Several moments of silence filled the phone. Verleen and Gracie used the coyote reference whenever one of them did not want to discuss a particular topic on the phone. Everyone in this neck of the woods knew that the Widow Comeaux spent her days watching the soaps on TV and listening in on her neighbors' conversations on the party line. Verleen thought she could hear her breathing in the background at that very moment.

"Do you have some of that lemon cake you're so famous for?" Gracie's casual tone was deliberate.

"Don't I always? I know how much everyone around here loves it."

"See you in a bit." Gracie hung up but Verleen continued to sit quietly with the phone to her ear until she heard a distant second click somewhere on the line. Once she returned her receiver to the wall, she allowed herself a chuckle. The Widow Comeaux seethed because Verleen's lemon cake took first prize two years ago at the county fair baking contest when the widow's cake didn't place at all.

"You're so fond of eavesdropping and then yapping about everyone's business all over the countryside, but I bet you won't be repeating that conversation," Verleen said out loud to the empty kitchen.

Glancing out the screen door, she noted that the little boy remained on the porch. Boone was lying on his back with his head in the boy's lap and was receiving an enthusiastic belly scratching. Verleen gave another chuckle and began preparing a fresh pot of coffee.

Ten minutes later, she heard a car pull up the drive just as she set the cake and coffee fixings on the table. She heard the front door open and Gracie's voice.

"I'm glad you called. I had just about talked myself into givin' my cupboards a good cleaning out. You saved me from that tedious chore. I'll put that aside for another day."

Gracie plopped down in a chair at the table and poured herself a cup of coffee, adding cream and sugar in generous amounts. Verleen set a piece of lemon cake in front of her long-time friend and took a chair herself. Gracie wasted no time in digging in. Although Verleen was a decade older than Gracie, they had become close friends from the first time they met and had remained so down through the years.

"You know, we really should invite the Widow Comeaux over for cake and coffee. Call her up right now," Gracie said around a mouthful.

"No, thank you. I'm sure that grouchy, old woman would love to get a look at the inside of my house and then go around lyin' and telling everyone my kitchen is a dirty pigsty," Verleen said with certainty.

"But it's the Christian thang to do...her being a widow and all," Gracie said feigning innocence but with a telling twinkle in her eye.

"Hummmp, don't talk to me about Christian charity. That old woman is still bitter 'cause the money she donated to the county fair committee didn't buy her a first place ribbon."

Gracie shoveled the last bite of cake into her mouth and laughed at Verleen's sour expression. "Want another piece?" Verleen asked.

"Maybe later." Gracie did love her sweets and her plump figure attested to that fact.

They both sipped coffee in quiet for a few seconds and then Verleen stood and crossed over to the sink. She glanced out the kitchen window and said, "I need to borrow some of little Henry's clothes."

"My grandson, little Henry?"

"Yep," Verleen said.

"Well, sure...I keep a drawer full of clothes for all the grandbabies for when they come to stay. Was this what you didn't want to talk about on the phone?" Gracie asked rather perplexed.

"Yep, and also this..." she answered simply and gestured out the kitchen window.

Carrying her cup with her, Gracie came to the sink and peered out.

"Land's sakes…who is that little feller?"

"You remember me mentioning my second cousin in Arkansas? Well, she has a daughter doing poorly, and I said I would take care of her grandson while she's nursing the boy's momma back to health."

Gracie nodded vaguely at Verleen's explanation.

"They didn't really send him much in the way of clothes."

"I'll go get some of Henry's right now," Gracie replied and headed for the door.

"Hold on a minute, Gracie. Sit back down."

Verleen looked out the window. The little boy, squatting in the yard, dug in a crawfish hole with a stick with Boone by his side. Satisfied that he was safe for the moment, Verleen resumed her seat at the dining table. Looking directly at her best friend she confessed, "That was a bald-faced lie. He's not my cousin's kid. I found that little boy in the edge of the woods yesterday."

Gracie stared at Verleen and her mouth opened and closed several times before she stuttered, "But…but why…I…I don't understand…why did you say?…" Her voice trailed off as her face displayed total confusion.

"I lied because I found him…and I'm gonna keep him."

Chapter 4

"If or when his parents come looking for him, he will be right here, safe and sound with me," Verleen continued.

"You can't just keep him like he's a nickel you found on the sidewalk," Gracie said in disapproval.

"Why not?"

"You just can't…you have to call someone…" Gracie sputtered.

"Just who do you recommend I call?" Verleen asked patiently.

"I don't know…the sheriff, perhaps."

"What's the county sheriff gonna do for this child?"

"Probably turn him over to an agency?" Gracie sounded uncertain.

"So they can stick him in some overcrowded, underfunded orphanage and forget about him? Oh, yeah, that's a **great** idea," Verleen replied with heavy sarcasm. "Nope, I can take good care of him and return him to his folks better than some government agency that will lose him in the shuffle," she continued determinedly.

"But if the authorities find out, you'll get into trouble."

"How are they gonna find out? You gonna turn me in?"

"Well, no…but don't you think people are gonna notice when this little feller is following you around?"

"I'm gonna tell 'em he's my second cousin's grandson…that lie slid right by you, didn't it? And you know me better than anyone."

Gracie had no argument for that. She shook her head worriedly. "I just don't want you to get into trouble, Verleen."

"Well, they are going to look pretty stupid for putting an old woman in jail 'cause she found a little boy in her back yard and decided to feed and clothe him until his parents showed up."

"I guess…" Gracie admitted uncertainly. "Has he said how he ended up lost or who his parents are?"

Verleen shook her head and took a sip of coffee.

"Well, what's his name? How old is he?"

Verleen just lifted one shoulder in a vague gesture and avoided her friend's eyes.

"Has he said anything at all?" Gracie's voice was rising in alarm.

"No, not a word," Verleen replied.

"Don't you think that's rather odd? There might be something wrong with him."

"I don't know, Gracie. Maybe he's been through something frightening and doesn't want to talk just yet."

"You suppose he's deaf or mute?"

"No, he can hear and he understands. He will talk when he's ready."

"Verleen, I just hope you're not biting off more than you can swallow."

"Don't you mean chew?"

"That's what I said."

"No, you said…oh, never mind, Gracie."

The screen door slammed causing them both to jump. Verleen looked around at the little boy standing in the doorway. "Come here and meet my best friend in the world. This here's Gracie. She lives up the road and is gonna let us borrow some clothes for you."

The boy came up beside Verleen and stood so close that she was able to slip her arm around him and hug him to her side. "The next time her grandkids come to stay, she'll bring them over and y'all can play in the yard. Won't that be fun?"

The little boy remained silent but stuck a finger in his mouth and looked shyly at Gracie.

"My goodness, little man, look at those dirty hands. I do believe you been busy making mud pies. Go give them a good scrubbing in the bathroom sink and then meet me in your room. I think I have a box of toys in the back of the closet somewhere. I'll dig them out for you."

As usual, he responded without a word and headed to the bathroom to do her bidding. Gracie's eyes followed him down the hall and then she looked at Verleen.

"If you expect people to believe he's your relative, he's gonna need a name."

"I been thinking about that. I think I'll call him Rowdy."

"Rowdy?" Gracie asked bewilderedly.

"Sure, see how he just bounces off the walls, tearing up the place, and wreaking havoc?" Verleen replied mockingly.

Gracie rolled her eyes, "Oh, Verleen, you have a warped sense of humor…you know that?"

"Better than no sense of humor…like the Widow Comeaux." And they both cracked up and laughed like the old friends that they truly were.

Sometime later, the boy sat on the bed in his room wearing the clothes Gracie brought over. Verleen finally found the old cardboard box of toys and had poured them out on the bed. Together they sorted through them. It was a hodge-podge assortment of small metal planes, trucks, and tractors and some plastic horses, cows, and other farm animals. While Verleen talked, the boy contentedly lined up the toys on the quilt, carefully examining each one as he did so.

"These were my Billy's toys," she said quietly.

The boy looked up quizzically.

"Billy was my son…my only child," she said in reply to the question on his face. She reached over to a shelf on the wall and picked up the framed photo of a young man in a military uniform. She sighed sadly before continuing, "He was killed in 1951in the Korean Conflict. He was only 18 and was called up right away when the draft began. He was so proud to go serve his country. My husband, Elmer, never quite got over losing him. I guess it's not something you can get over." She sat looking at the photo for several seconds before she spoke again.

"A stroke took Elmer ten years ago so it's just been me on the farm for a while now." Verleen felt herself slipping into the past with all its pain and sorrow so she shook herself mentally and brushed at the tears that threatened in her eyes. She looked around the room with its baseball pennants on the wall and sports trophies on the shelves, a room that still looked much the same as when Billy occupied it.

"This is your room now while you're here and you can stay as long as you want."

The boy stopped playing with the toys when she started speaking of Billy and listened intently. With a look of grave sympathy, he reached up and softly patted her cheek as if to offer comfort. Verleen looked down into the depths of his brown eyes and said, "I swear…I think you're much older than you appear."

Hearing that, the boy dropped his eyes away from hers and began noiselessly playing with the toys again. The spell broken, Verleen blinked her eyes and looked around the room. *Sometimes I let my imagination get the best of me. He's just a lost, scared, little boy.* Placing Billy's photo back on the shelf, she headed out the door. "I've still got some chores to do and this day is getting away from me."

The boy followed Verleen around the small farm as she finished up the last few daily tasks. He carried the egg basket as she reached under the laying hens for their treasures, and he peeked into a few of the unoccupied nests finding still-warm eggs nestled there. When Verleen paused in the back yard to point out where the vegetables would soon be planted, he listened attentively to her future plans for the garden.

Leaving the boy on the porch with Boone, Verleen went into the kitchen and hastily made some sandwiches for lunch. Sitting side-by-side on the back porch steps, they devoured the sandwiches, washed them down with sweet tea, and topped off their meal with homemade oatmeal cookies. The porch was a relaxing place to sit, and the surrounding forest made a pleasant view as the day continued to warm.

"We've probably had our last frost before spring. I'm ready for sunshiny days and green leaves on the trees again." Verleen smiled down at the little boy. She continued, "You know, I been thinking. I just can't call you 'little man'. What do your folks call you?"

The boy shared his last bite of cookie with Boone and continued to rub the old dog's head as if he hadn't heard the question but Verleen knew that he had. "I reckon we need a name for you. Do you have any suggestions? No? Then how 'bout Boone?" That got the boy's attention. He gave her a look that said, "Are you serious?"

Verleen shook her head. "No, that won't work. That's the dog's name and that will just cause confusion," she said with exaggerated seriousness. "Now let me think. How 'bout Octavius? No, that's a mighty big name for a little boy. Chauncy?... doesn't sound right. Hmmm…Woodrow? Nope, you just don't look like a Woodrow. Minerva?...that's a girl's name so that just won't do."

Verleen continued for several minutes with a list of ridiculous names that began to bring a slight smile to the boy's face. "If you have any ideas, nows the time to let me know." But the boy maintained his silence, seemingly content to be entertained by her comical suggestions.

"How do you feel about Calvin? That was my great-granddaddy's name."

Turning his attention back to Boone, the boy gave a slight shrug and Verleen took that as a sign he was agreeable. "Calvin," she said slowly, trying it out. "Yep, I think that's the one." *The name does seem to suit him and I guess if he doesn't like it, he will let me know what he'd rather be called.*

For the rest of the day, the boy shadowed Verleen as she went about her normal activities. Late evening found the two of them sitting on the couch in front of the television in the living room. The boy was fresh from his bath and attired in some of Henry's pajamas while Verleen lounged in her house robe. The national news was on and Verleen was surprised to find the boy glued to the program. The news program was mostly devoted to the subject of the Vietnam War and the supposed withdrawal of American troops.

Verleen watched the broadcast with a heavy heart. *So many lives lost. There's no winners in this war. It's time our boys came home.*

When the news signed off, she encouraged the boy to find something else to watch. "Change the channel to something entertaining. There's only three channels but sometimes if you adjust those rabbit ears on top of the set, you might pick up a station out of Louisiana."

The boy climbed off the couch and obediently turned the channel on the front of the television. Each time he found a station, he would pause and look back at Verleen for a second before turning to the next station.

"Oh, honey, watch whatever you like. I don't care about most of that foolishness they have on nowadays. I mostly turn it on for the news."

The boy eventually settled on a western program and returned to sit on the couch beside Verleen who had her feet propped up on an ottoman and was knitting with bright green yarn. As the night deepened outside the little farm house, the Cartwrights chased bad guys across the TV screen and the boy, now called Calvin, fell soundly asleep to the sounds of gunfights, running horses, and the soft clicking of knitting needles.

Chapter 5

"Calvin, are you ready?" Verleen asked as she sat down in a kitchen chair to slip on her shoes. Looking up she spied the boy standing in the hallway. He was dressed in jeans, tennis shoes, and a T-shirt, all courtesy of Gracie's little Henry. Picking up her purse, she headed out the front door. "Grab that basket of eggs on the table, will ya'? Be real easy with them."

Opening the door of her old 1955 stepside Chevy truck, she glanced around. Calvin was standing on the porch, holding the basket. "Well, come on, honey. Let's get going."

Calvin didn't move. He seemed to be rooted to the top step.

"It's my egg delivery day. We're just going down to Miller's Mercantile. It will be alright. You'll see." This would be Calvin's first time to leave the safety and seclusion of Verleen's farm. She could clearly sense his reluctance. She left the truck door open, climbed the porch steps, and sat down on the top one. "It's okay, Calvin. I know you're scared, but I won't let anything happen to you. Everyone's gonna think you're my family and you don't have to talk to anyone if you don't want to. You think you can trust old Nana Vee to keep you safe?"

After a several quiet seconds, the boy looked directly into Verleen's eyes and nodded. "Good...the sooner we make this delivery, the sooner we can come home." She took Calvin by the hand and led him to the truck. After settling him into the truck on the seat beside her, she handed him the egg basket to hold in his lap. "Alright, you are now keeper of the egg basket. Hold onto it with both hands and don't let any of them crack."

Starting up her old truck, she backed up in the yard and headed down the dirt driveway. As she reached the county road, she turned right and drove to the small settlement of Lolly Springs. It couldn't really be called more than a settlement or community since it consisted only of a post office, a mercantile, a barber shop, a small sub-courthouse, a feed store, and a few other small businesses. Its original name was Loblolly Springs due to the tall loblolly pine forest in the surrounding countryside, but with Texans' lazy way of speaking and their habit of dropping the beginning or ending of words, it had been shortened to

Lolly Springs years ago. The next town of any size was Berryville 25 miles further down the highway. Verleen pulled into a spot in front of the mercantile and put the truck in park. With the basket in one hand and holding onto Calvin's hand with the other, she pushed opened the squeaky screen door of the store and stepped inside. The four or five customers that browsed the shelves voiced a greeting to Verleen and she smiled and waved as she headed to the counter.

"Good morning, Miz Verleen. Who's that young man you've got with you today?" asked the tall, middle-aged man behind the counter.

"This is Calvin, my second cousin's grandson. He's come to stay with me for a bit," Verleen answered casually and launched right into her reason for being in the store. "You'll be glad to know that my hens have really stepped up production and I have a good many eggs for you this week." She set the basket of eggs on the counter and waited expectantly.

"That's mighty fine, Miz Verleen. You want cash or did you want to swap it for goods?"

"Cash will be fine."

She waited as the man counted the eggs in the basket, pulled money from the register, and laid it on the counter in front of her. She started to scoop it up but then paused. Looking up at the big man she spoke in a quiet voice, "Uh, Pete…I think you shortchanged me some."

Pete looked down at the money on the counter and said, "Nope, it's correct."

"But you always pay me 30 cents a dozen and I brought you four and a half dozen today," she said puzzled.

"Oh, I'm only going to be paying 20 cents from now on," he replied. "The cost of overhead going up and all…you know," he said airily with a small smirk.

"Your overhead on eggs being exactly what?" Verleen said in a tight voice. "You don't house the chickens or buy the chicken feed and I deliver the eggs to you." She looked at the price list on the wall behind him. "I see you're now charging the customers 55 cents a dozen instead of the usual 45 cents, and you know full well that people will have to drive all the way over to Berryville and catch them on sale to get a decent price."

Her voice had begun to rise and the customers were now craning their necks to see what was going on at the counter. She stood silently for several seconds taking in his arrogant posture. "You know…people around here have always hinted that you're the greedy type, but I didn't want to believe it. I see it now. You're trying to rip me off along with all the nice folks of this community, too."

Pete folded his arms over his chest and his smirk became more pronounced. "Miz Verleen, you just take your money and run along now. If people don't like my prices, they can take their business elsewhere," he announced loudly.

"You know, Pete, you old tightwad, you're exactly right. I **will** take my business elsewhere…and my eggs, too." Verleen snatched the basket off the counter so quickly that two of the eggs landed on the floor and cracked, oozing yellow yolks.

"Hey, you're making a mess!" Pete's smirk was gone.

Verleen grabbed Calvin's hand and headed for the front of the store. She carelessly bumped the basket against the end of a shelf as she walked by and three more eggs burst as they hit the floor. Pausing as she neared an elderly couple in the center aisle, she spoke in a friendly tone, "Good morning, Mr. and Mrs. Jenkins, would you like some free eggs today?"

"Verleen Jackson, you can't do that!" Pete yelled from where he still stood behind the counter. His neck flushed a bright red that began climbing to his face.

"Watch me!" Verleen shot back.

She began handing eggs to the elderly couple who were putting them into their pockets. Other customers also hurried over to get free eggs.

Verleen plastered a smile on her face as she explained pleasantly, "These eggs are fresh off my farm and free today as a promotion to announce my new business. I'll be selling them from my house from now on. Only 40 cents a dozen! You can find me on Old Hickory Road

and sometimes out on the highway selling vegetables out of the back of my truck. I might even set up a table right down the street here on the sidewalk. Tell your friends about me now, won't you?"

Mr. Tightwad was now descending into a conniption fit and threatening to call the police.

Verleen just snickered and looked around at the other customers who now seemed to be less enthused about shopping at the mercantile. "I don't know about y'all but I'll be doing my grocery shopping in

Berryville from now on. Pete here won't be getting any of my money." As she and Calvin sailed out the door, she threw a parting shot over her shoulder. "Go ahead and call Constable Boyd and tell him he needs to lock me up for giving away free eggs!" She hooted with laughter that continued as she reached the truck.

A few minutes later, she was puttering down the dusty county road still having a chuckle or two. "Did you see his face when those eggs hit the floor? Greedy, old fool thought I'd stand for being cheated. He didn't realize that he was actually doing me a favor. I'll make more money now and my customers will pay less. We'll just cut out the middle man. Should have done it a long time ago. Folks 'round here don't make much money and they are stretched thin as it is."

Glancing down, she saw Calvin's unsmiling face as he sat clutching the basket. The breeze coming through the rolled-down windows ruffled his brown curls. "There's a life lesson for you, little man. Sometimes, you have to stand up for yourself and not let others intimidate you. Looks like we still have a few eggs left in the basket and I know just what to do with them." Turning the truck down an overgrown lane, Verleen followed the driveway that wound through tall standing pines and overgrown grass finally coming to a stop in front of a dilapidated house with peeling paint. The house looked tired and rickety. The porch was sagging and the roof was badly in need of repair. It was obvious that the owners had given up and so had the house.

"Wait here, Calvin." While Verleen approached the house carrying the basket, the little boy knelt on the seat and watched through the open truck window. "Sally?" she called as she climbed the steps to the porch.

A blonde woman appeared on the other side of the screen door. She carried a baby on her hip and a toddler hung onto her shirt tail. She had probably been pretty once, but now she looked as weary and shabby as the house she occupied.

"Hey, Miz Verleen, come on in. The house is a mess. I'd have straightened up some had I known you was coming by."

"I can't stay. I just wanted to stop by and drop off these fresh eggs. You and the kids doing alright?"

"We're fine. The little one here has had an earache but other than that..." her voice trailed off.

"Where are the twins?"

"They went hunting for rabbits but I expect them back anytime."

"As soon as they get back, you send one of them around to my house. I'm cooking up a big pot of gumbo for supper and there'll be too much for me and Old John to eat all by ourselves. I'll send you and the kids some."

"Miz Verleen, you don't have to do that…" Sally sounded flustered.

"Well, it will just go to waste 'cause I always cook so much. There's no such thing as making a small pot of gumbo. I'll look for one of the boys before dark. You send him 'round, now, you hear?"

"Yes, ma'am, I sure appreciate it," Sally replied gratefully.

Reaching the truck, Verleen said, "If you and the kids need anything, you let me know." She climbed in, started the engine, and reversed in the yard. Waving out the window, she and Calvin headed back down the driveway.

"Did you hear that, Calvin? We are cooking up a gumbo for supper." Slipping into a Cajun accent, she said, "I sho' do love me a good gumbo, sha."

A glance down at Calvin's face had her laughing out loud. He had cut his eyes to the side in her direction and was looking at her skeptically as if he did not know her.

"I take it that you have never had gumbo?" she asked in her normal voice. Calvin just shrugged slightly as if to say he didn't know.

"Well, I'm gonna introduce you to something that my momma taught me how to make. We are so far southeast in Texas, that we are almost in Louisiana…and dats where my people come from," she said slipping into the Cajun accent again. "Wid a little of dis and a little of dat, we gonna cook up a big, fine gumbo, fo' sho'."

Chapter 6

As Verleen added a pitcher of water to the browned flour, a cloud of steam erupted from the pot with a loud hiss. She stirred the water and flour together until it was smooth, her face beading with perspiration in the process. "That was the tricky part, getting the roux dark, dark brown and stopping just this side of burning it. Got to use a really good gumbo pot or you can burn the bottom clean out of just any old pan." She continued to stir the ingredients for several minutes. "It's time to add the Holy Trinity…the onions, bell peppers, and celery." She dumped the chopped vegetables into the pot and wiped her hands on her apron. "Now we'll let it simmer a while."

She glanced over at Calvin who was watching her with interest. "How are those cookies coming?" He stood on a kitchen chair wearing an apron tied up so high it was under his armpits. He held the ring from a mason jar lid that served as a cookie cutter and had flour on most of his face. After she rolled out the molasses cookie dough on the counter, she had put him to work cutting out the cookies while she started the gumbo.

She smothered a smile as she took in his white-powdered features. "I do love a man that throws himself into his work," she said. Leaning against the cabinet next to him, she surveyed his efforts. There were misshapen forms on the cookie sheet that vaguely resembled the round ring. "Would you by chance have eaten a few bites of cookie dough?"

Calvin's eyes grew serious as he avoided her direct gaze and looked down at the flat dough on the counter. "That's the best part of making cookies but don't tell anybody," Verleen said, and she pinched off a large chunk of dough from the bowl and popped it into her mouth.

Calvin broke into a grin and resumed cutting out deformed circles until the pan was full, and Verleen slid it into the warm oven. They worked together until all the cookies were baked and cooling on the counter, and Verleen added the chicken and sausage to the gumbo which bubbled merrily on the back burner of the stove. She washed the dirty dishes while Calvin stood on his chair at the sink and took on the job of rinsing and stacking them in the drain board.

Verleen wiped the flour from Calvin's face, fixed them both a glass of sweet tea, and they sat down at their customary places at the table, Verleen at the end closest to the stove and Calvin opposite her on his overturned pot that served as a booster seat. They sipped and enjoyed a warm-from-the-oven cookie. "Shoo! I had to sit down a minute. My dogs are barking!"

Calvin tilted his head and looked at her and then at the back screen door, his expression clearly puzzled. "Oh, I didn't mean Boone. I meant my feet hurt. Haven't you ever heard anybody say that?" Calvin shook his head as he drank his tea. "Have you ever had molasses cookies before or gumbo?" Calvin shrugged his shoulders in what was becoming his signature response and then shook his head again. "Just where did you come from, my little man?" she asked very softly. Calvin ignored the question and continued to nibble his snack.

Verleen snapped her fingers loudly causing Calvin to look up. "I know…I just figured it out. You grew in my garden. That's why you were so dirty when I found you. I bet you popped up out of the ground between the tators and the carrots…or maybe…you fell out of a robin's nest. Yeah, that's it…" Verleen put a thoughtful expression on her face, "But you don't have wings so that don't make sense…" Wrinkling her brow and squinting her eyes, she asked "Did the forest fairies snatch you and leave you in my yard?"

Calvin was grinning from ear-to-ear now, clearly enjoying Verleen's teasing. "I've got it! I've got it! I knowed what happened. You're a coyote cub that got separated from the pack. That's why they are howling all times of the night out in the woods. Aaaaoooo!" Verleen was howling and Calvin was giggling and shaking his head. "Aaaaoooo, yip yip yip! Come home, Calvin! Aaaaaaooooo!"

To her amazement, the normally silent child began howling along with her. When a third howling voice chimed in, they turned to the screen door where Boone sat on the porch joining the howling chorus, and Verleen and Calvin laughed so hard they almost choked on their cookies.

When their laughter died down, they took their glasses of tea out onto the back porch. Verleen rocked while Calvin sat on the wooden plank floor playing with his toys. She watched as he lined up his trucks and airplanes and became lost in a make-believe world to which only little children are privy. Smiling, she opened the newspaper that came from Berryville and thumbed through the articles looking for news that caught her interest.

"Looks like Charley Pride won a Grammy for best country male performer. He sure can sing. He's right up there with Patsy Cline or Bob Wills. Now that there is what real music sounds like…" Calvin continued to run his cars across the porch planks as she rambled aloud about the daily news. "I see flour and sugar are going on sale next week at Thrif-Tee's and on Tuesday they give double S & H green stamps so that's the best day to go. We'll have to make a run over to Berryville and stock up. The IRA is still exploding bombs in London and killing people." Verleen shook her head sadly. "Fighting over territory and religion. That has been going on since the beginning of time. You'd think they would get tired of all the strife and dying." She glanced down at Calvin who had now paused in his play and was looking up at her with a serious expression. "Guess that's not really a topic for a young boy," she mumbled to herself. Turning the page, she continued to peruse the articles. "The paper says they're getting ready to send a space station up into orbit. Wonder what's the purpose in all that?" she asked aloud.

As usual, her question went unanswered and when she glanced at him, the boy appeared to be staring off into the distance. "They put a man on the moon a few years ago…or at least they said they did. Some folks think it's just a government hoax. Imagine…a man walkin' on the moon." She shook her head and sighed, "I don't know about all that. I got enough to do right here. Can't imagine going lookin' for some new spot in the universe to take care of. Be my luck, there would be space chickens to feed and moon dust somebody would be expectin' me to clean. I supposed they would be needin' me to make cheese and butter out of the Milky Way."

Calvin seemed not to have heard her joking remarks. "Calvin?" she said. "Honey, you okay?" For a few seconds longer, he continued to stare into space and then he slowly turned his face to hers. He smiled briefly and then resumed playing with his toys as she picked up the paper again and began turning pages. *Still waters run deep but Lord only knows what thoughts are flitting around in his little mind. Guess he'll let me in on them when he's good and ready.*

Later, Calvin set the table while Verleen put the finishing touches to the gumbo. She stirred in chopped green onion and seasonings. There was a rustle on the back porch and Verleen told Calvin, "Set another place. Mistah John will be joining us."

Calvin stood still and looked at Verleen in surprise. "Go on now," she chided gently. "Mistah John is a good friend of mine. You'll like him. Although, I don't think I'll be able to get a word in edgewise this afternoon with you two chatterboxes at the table." A little louder toward the back door she said, "We got us a gumbo today, Mistah John. Come on in."

The screen door squeaked as he stepped into the kitchen. He stopped and looked at Calvin who was rooted in place staring right back. "Calvin, meet Mistah John. Mistah John, Calvin. This little feller is stayin' with me for a while. He sure has been a big help around the farm. Don't know what I did without him before," she said throwing a wink at the old gentleman.

Her words prompted Calvin into motion and he began to add another glass and utensils to the table as Verleen dished up rice and gumbo in big bowls. When everyone had been served and seated and grace had been given, she passed a bowl of potato salad around. While Calvin watched, Old John plopped a big spoonful of the cold salad onto the wide ledge of his soup bowl. The little boy glanced quizzically at Verleen who put her potato salad onto a small side plate. She answered Calvin's silent query, "There's no right way to eat it. Everyone has their own preference."

Calvin put a small spoonful on his side plate and then another on the soup bowl ledge just as Old John had done. Watching the older man, he copied his way of loading his spoon with both salad and gumbo and after tasting it, he hesitated no longer.

"I think dis young man knows a good thing when he finds it," Old John chuckled.

When the old man added some Tabasco to his bowl, Calvin started to do the same.

"Hold on there, Calvin. That stuff will scorch your mouth. You'd better try a drop first and see if you can handle the heat," Verleen advised.

Calvin put several drops on his spoon and popped it into his mouth before she could slow him down. Instead of catching his breath and making blowing noises as she expected, he just licked his lips and shook a goodly amount into his gumbo and proceeded to eat with enthusiasm.

Old John chuckled and shook his head. "I do believe Calvin is pure-bred Cajun."

Verleen nodded in agreement. "Calvin, would your last name be Boudreaux, Broussard, or Guidry?"

The little boy just lifted his shoulders and shook his head as he gobbled up his gumbo and potato salad.

"What about Benoit, Fontenot, or Landry?" she continued as Old John's grin grew larger.

"Don't give away all yo' secrets, Calvin," Old John said in a loud whisper.

"No chance of that. Secrets he's got…and plenty of them," Verleen said dryly.

For the next several minutes the only sound in the kitchen was the scraping of spoons in bowls as they enjoyed their supper until a knock sounded at the back door.

Chapter 7

Verleen twisted around in her chair and spotted a young man on the other side of the screen door. "Come on in here, Jimmy. I was just thinking it was about time for you to come by." The teenager stepped into the kitchen, taking off his ball cap as he did so.

"Momma said I was to run over to fetch something, Nana Vee. I'm sorry to be interrupting your supper. I can just wait out on the porch."

"You will do no such thing. You just set right down here and have a bowl of gumbo." As she spoke she was already dishing up a serving for him and pulling out a chair.

"I really should be getting back…" he protested weakly.

She poured him a glass of ice tea, ignoring his objection.

"Dig in, Jimmy. Foods done been blessed." She took her seat and Jimmy sat down obediently. Picking up his spoon, he began to eat as though ravenous. "Did you and Timmy get many rabbits today?"

"One or two," he said around bites of food. Verleen placed a plate of potato salad beside his bowl and refilled his ice tea glass which was already empty.

"He sho' likes yo' gumbo, Miz Vee," Old John said softly.

Jimmy nodded in agreement, his mouth too full of food to answer. When he attacked the potato salad, Verleen refilled his bowl with gumbo and he smiled his thanks. His initial hunger satiated, he dug into the second helping at a slower pace.

"How's the baby's earache?" Verleen asked.

"Better," he said in between spoonfuls.

"And little Ivy? How she doin'?"

"Startin' to talk up a storm and followin' me and Timmy everywhere we go," he said with a small smile.

"And your daddy? He been home much?" she asked casually.

Jimmy ate several bites before he answered. "Ain't seen him in 'bout a week," he said flatly, looking down at the table.

And ain't had no groceries in the house for a week either, I bet. When he's there, drunk and hung-over, he's probably making their lives all kinds of living hell and when he's gone, they're left broke and hungry.

"Have you tried gettin' some work to help out?" Verleen asked quietly.

Jimmy halted the spoon's path to his mouth and looked directly at Verleen. "I've tried, Nana Vee, but nobody's hiring a 14 year old...especially if you're Grady Turner's son." The words were spoken with a sour tinge and Verleen nodded sympathetically.

Calvin had stopped eating when Jimmy had joined the table and his big, brown eyes darted nervously between Old John and the teenager. *I guess two new strangers at the same time are just a little much for him to handle.* "Calvin, pass the crackers to our guests."

Calvin turned his steady gaze to her. She smiled encouragingly as he timidly slid the bowl of crackers across the table to Jimmy. "This here's my cousin's grandson. He's gonna stay awhile and help me in my garden this summer."

Jimmy nodded acknowledgement in Calvin's general direction and Verleen supposed a four-year old was really of little interest to him. She then steered the conversation to safer subjects for the remainder of the meal...what conversation there was. Old John said little and Calvin, as usual, nothing at all. Jimmy had, like everyone else, accepted her brief explanation of Calvin's identity without question and was more interested in supper than chatting.

At the end of the meal and with some strong prompting, Calvin grabbed the plate of molasses cookies from the counter and proudly went around the table serving them while Verleen explained how the boy had played a big part in their creation. His little face beamed when the dinner guests proclaimed them delicious and asked for more.

Verleen took in the sight of her dining table surrounded by familiar faces and felt a sense of satisfaction that she now realized had eluded her for some time. *I guess family comes in all shapes and sizes and kinfolks are who you want them to be.*

While Jimmy quickly ate half a dozen cookies, Verleen dished up rice, gumbo, potato salad, and molasses cookies into containers for his family. He made a quick exit as soon as she had it ready, and she surmised that Sally and the rest of the kids were most likely as hungry as Jimmy had been.

Unlike the teenager, Old John slowly savored his cookies with the coffee Verleen served. "Mighty fine cookies, young man, mighty fine. Anytime you wanna practice yo' baking skills, I be proud to be the taster." Calvin smiled broadly in response and then shyly looked down at the table.

"Do you think you can take a look at the roof of the lean-to out at the barn before it gets dark? I think there's a leak and I sure would hate it if the sacks of cow feed got wet and ruined the next time it rains."

"I surely will do that right now," Old John replied. He rose from the table and headed for the back door. Pausing and turning back, he spoke to Calvin, "Come along, little feller. I might needs you to hold the ladder." Calvin hesitated so Verleen prodded him, "Go on, now. Give Mistah John a hand."

Calvin slipped from the table and looked back over his shoulder at Verleen as he left the kitchen. She gave him what she hoped was an encouraging smile, and watched from the window over the sink as they headed across the yard to the barn. As she washed up the dishes and put the kitchen in order, the sunlight slowly began to fade outside. Verleen felt right pleased that Calvin had made a new friend.

The days began to slip by and Verleen was surprised to realize one morning that Calvin had been with her for about a month. Spring was coming on as the days and nights warmed helping winter become a thing of the past; together the two companions slipped into a comfortable routine on the farm. It hadn't taken long for people to find out that Verleen had moved her egg business to her house, and they showed up quite regularly to purchase the fresh eggs that the chickens were happily producing. Many of the locals didn't feel all that loyal to Pete down at the mercantile, apparently…either that or they really needed to save 15 cents. Verleen figured it was a little of each. Coincidentally, Bessie had begun producing so much milk lately that Verleen was seriously thinking about expanding her business by offering milk, cream, and homemade butter to her customers as well.

Calvin took over the daily egg gathering and the feeding and watering of the chickens, and he seemed to enjoy those chores never needing reminding. He fetched a small basket right after breakfast each morning and headed out to the chicken pen returning with the basket brimming with eggs. Pulling a chair up to the kitchen table, he carefully transferred the eggs to empty cardboard cartons that the customers brought back to be refilled. He was intent on his job and very few eggs were dropped or cracked.

Verleen, Calvin, and Old John began work on the spring garden by using the old push plow to cultivate the dirt, and together they carried buckets of cow manure to work into the soil to make it rich and fertile. Using hoes and rakes, they broke up the large clods of earth and removed any grass or weeds before finally mounding it up into neat rows. As Verleen poked indentions into the dirt with the end of the hoe handle, Calvin followed behind dropping seeds in the holes. They worked well as a team planting and watering the seeds, and Calvin seemed to enjoy gardening as much as Verleen. They planted onions, peas, potatoes, turnips, and spinach with plans to sow other vegetables in the weeks to come. Meanwhile, the little boy developed a habit of going out several times a day to check the garden for the first signs of the seedlings pushing up through the soil.

Today, Verleen sat on the back porch surveying her neat garden, taking in the orderly rows that, for now, were free of weeds. "More coffee?" she asked Gracie.

"I think I'll have another cup and another one of those molasses cookies, if you don't mind," Gracie answered.

Verleen returned quickly after having filled their cups once again in the kitchen and placed a saucer of cookies on the small table between their rocking chairs on the porch. They munched in silence for several minutes and watched Calvin swinging gleefully on the new tire swing hanging from the limb of the tall sycamore tree in the yard. The bright green, knitted cap that Verleen had quickly completed now covered his brown curls.

"Where did Old John find that tire for the swing, Verleen?"

"Beats me…he just came walking down the path one morning rolling it in front of him. I had some rope in the barn and within a matter of minutes Calvin was climbing all over that thing like a monkey."

"He sure seems to be enjoying himself." Gracie nodded in Calvin's direction. The boy had moved from sitting on top of the tire to lying in the hole in the middle with his arms and legs spread wide as if imitating a soaring airplane. If the sounds he made were any indication, that's exactly what he pretended to be as he sailed back and forth through the air.

"He sure acts like a typical little boy…except for the lack of talking. Lord have mercy, my grandkids wake up every morning all full of questions…just follow me around throughout the day talking up a blue sky and-"

"Not sky…streak," Verleen interrupted.

"What?" Gracie looked puzzled.

"The expression is…talking up a blue **streak**," Verleen answered.

"Okay, Verleen…I'm just trying to say that my grandkids never run out of things to talk about and it's really odd how Calvin never says a word."

"I'll admit that it worries me, too, but I can't force him to talk and pressuring him won't help. I just know that he will talk when he is good and ready," she said with certainty.

"Any idea about who that boy might belong to?"

Verleen shook her head. "That's the strangest thing, Gracie. I haven't heard the slightest talk from anyone about a missing child…not in the papers, not on the local TV news…not even a peep in town or from the surrounding communities. I just don't understand how someone can lose their child and never bother to mention it. What kind of people are we talking about?"

"It is so strange, isn't it?" Gracie agreed. "If one of my children or grandchildren came up missing, I would be screaming my head off…scouring the woods, knocking on doors…and forming search parties. I'd be doing something…anything until they were found."

"You and me both, sister," Verleen agreed firmly. "Seems to me if you can't take better care of your child than that, he's better off with someone else who will."

"Lord knows that's true," Gracie agreed quietly.

"I take it my little, white lie about him being a distant relative of mine has caused no suspicion from the folks hereabouts?"

"None whatsoever…although the fact that you can look people straight in the face and tell a lie as slick as grease makes me wonder if I really know you at all, Verleen."

"What can I say, Gracie? We all have our own unique, God-given talents. Mine just happens to be inventing convincing stories. I can't help that people want to believe them," she replied in an exaggerated tone with a mocking smile.

"Verleen, don't be dragging God into this…that's just blasphemous. You know lying is a sin and-"

"Oh, pipe down. I'm just funnin' ya'. You know I'm only trying to protect that little boy out there."

"I know…I know," Gracie said with a half smile. "And as your oldest and dearest friend, you know that your secret is safe with me. I won't spill the cats out of the bag."

Verleen gave Gracie a long, exasperated look. Speaking slowly she said, "It's spill the beans **OR** let the cat out of the bag, Gracie. Talking to you can be so frustrating sometimes…you know that?"

Her friend rolled her eyes and said under her breath, "Look who's calling the teapot black."

Chapter 8

"Lucky you came by this morning, Lewis. You just bought the last of my eggs," Verleen told the man in the car as she handed him the carton through his window. The man tipped his hat and reversed his vehicle. "Tell Mable I hope her gout gets better."

"Will do!" the man said as he headed down the driveway.

"Guess we ought to go hang up our 'Sold Out' sign, Calvin," Verleen said to the little boy sitting on the front porch steps.

Calvin disappeared into the house only to return a few seconds later holding the piece of wood displaying the painted words. Together they walked to the end of the driveway that met the county road. The boy hung the sign on the hooks that were mounted under the wooden frame that held a sign proclaiming 'Fresh Eggs for Sale'.

"Stingy Pete at the mercantile did me a big favor when he tried to go back on our original arrangement. Don't know why I didn't do this from the start. Now I get to chat with folks from hereabouts when they drop by for eggs while putting more of the profit in my pocket, and my customers are getting the freshest eggs at a better price. I reckon I should send Stingy Pete an egg custard and a thank-you card!"

Calvin looked up at her in surprise.

"That was a joke, Calvin. Boy, we have got to get you a sense of humor. Maybe I'll make enough egg money so that we can drive over to the Thrif-Tee Market in Berryville and buy you one."

For several seconds, his face held its solemn, puzzled expression and then one corner of his mouth began to lift. A small snicker escaped as his mouth twisted sideways to try and contain the beginnings of a grin. As Verleen headed back toward the house, she heard giggles coming from behind and found herself chuckling out loud as well. Strolling back the way they came, the sun shone brightly through the bare limbs of the trees lining the lane.

Pointing at a few particular trees, she said, "Look at the redbud trees so full of color. They always show up to the party early with their tiny, pink blossoms and soon the rest of the trees will start putting out leaf buds. Then they'll all be greening up and covered in new leaves. Spring is a time for the earth to wake up and get dressed in a new outfit."

As they reached the porch, an unfamiliar car came rolling up the driveway. "Calvin, go inside and let me see who this is," Verleen said softly. "Don't come out unless I tell you to."

The boy obediently slipped into the house out of sight as a shiny, black car came to a stop.

A tall, lanky man in a dark suit climbed out of the vehicle just as the sun ducked behind a passing cloud casting the yard in shade. She looked him over carefully noting his hawkish nose and his oiled hair slicked down to his head. The man surveyed the yard and surrounding forest with a deliberate casual manner. "Mornin', ma'am. Miz Jackson I take it?"

"That's correct. Can I help you?"

"Well, I've been hearing about your egg business and thought I'd stop buy and pick up a few dozen."

"Sorry, I've sold out today," Verleen replied. "Guess you didn't see the sign at the end of my driveway."

"Oh, I did but I wanted to stop by anyway and introduce myself. I'm Devlin Connors, the new pastor at the Faith Believers Chapel here in Lolly Springs." The smile he had pasted on his face reminded Verleen of a used car salesman eager to strike a bargain, and his voice had that unmistakable southern preacher sound as if he were addressing a large crowd.

She remained silent and kept a neutral expression on her face. *Guess he'll get to the point if I just stand here.*

"I just wanted to stop by and invite you to my church, Miz Jackson," he said hastily.

The man's self-assured smile faltered a bit when Verleen made no comment in return and let the silence stretch on. "Nice little farm you have here." He turned around as he glanced about at the house and surrounding yard. His fake smile was back and pasted firmly in place as he faced her once again. "Yessiree, a real nice place. Neat as a pin."

"I have something on the stove I need to get back to---"

The man interrupted quickly, "I just think you would benefit from attending my church and wanted to extend a personal invitation."

MY church...interesting choice of words. "Thanks for stopping by," Verleen said quietly but firmly as she turned toward the door. She slipped inside and latched the screen door, cutting off any chance of further conversation. She watched from the dim inside of the house as the preacher stood by his car obviously flustered by her flat response and lack of welcoming reaction that he obviously expected. His prying eyes took one more look around Verleen's property and then he slid into his car. His face wore a scowl as he reversed and shot down the driveway.

Calvin hovered in the kitchen doorway wearing a worried expression.

"Not to worry, little man. I don't think he'll be back. He wasn't looking for you anyway. He give you the same uneasy feeling I got?"

Calvin nodded soberly.

"I learned a long time ago to always go with my instinct and it's never led me wrong. Times I went against it was times I regretted. Do you understand what I'm saying, Calvin? Always listen to that little voice inside." She peered into his face wondering if he could truly grasp her meaning.

He nodded slowly and she could only hope that he was old enough to comprehend.

"Good. Why don't you go fill up Boone's food bowl and then play in the back yard while I start the laundry?"

As Verleen crossed to the kitchen table and picked up her coffee cup, he scampered out the back door like the child he was, just happy to go frolic in the sunshine. Leaning against the sink, she sipped her now cold coffee and watched Calvin tossing an old tennis ball against the shed wall. Each time it bounced off the wall, Boone pounced on it and Calvin had to wrestle him down to get it back. Both seemed happy with the rules of the game and as Verleen watched, her disturbing visitor was quickly forgotten.

The days continued to warm and they finished planting the garden with okra, green beans, watermelons, squash, and corn. Calvin had taken delight in finding the first small seedlings of the earlier planting as they poked their heads up from the dirt. "Looks like we might have an abundance of vegetables this year. That means we will have plenty to share and sell," Verleen remarked. "That is if Boone will do his job and keep the deer out of the garden patch." They both looked at the dog who sat in a grassy spot and he barked in answer. Boone, well been trained in the past, stayed out of the plowed area, but when they worked the garden he always kept his vigil waiting at the end of the rows. "Okay, Calvin, we wait for the sun and rain to make it grow. If the rain doesn't come, we water it with the hose and then God will do the rest." Calvin looked at the garden and smiled in satisfaction. As Verleen headed to the shed with the gardening tools, she gently tugged his knitted cap down to cover his eyes and she heard him giggle at her jest.

Later that week, a soft, spring rain came to water the garden. The raindrops pattered softly on the back steps and thunder could be heard rolling in the distance. Calvin sat cross-legged on the floor gazing at the back yard through the screen door. It started drizzling during the night and had continued throughout the entire day. It was dark and gloomy outside with the sun failing to put in an appearance.

Verleen stepped up to the door behind Calvin and looked across the wet back yard also. "No use keepin' an eye out. Mistah John doesn't venture out in weather like this. He won't be around for supper today but he'll be back in a few days. Don't you worry none." She crossed the kitchen and sat down at table. "Come here, Calvin. I have something to show you."

The little boy took one last, long look out at the rain, rose reluctantly, and took a seat in a kitchen chair. He looked at the object Verleen had set on the table and then looked at her questioningly.

"Well, what do you think?" she asked.

Calvin just shrugged.

"Don't you know what it is?"

Calvin shook his head and wrinkled his brow in perplexion.

Verleen gestured to the bright pink, porcelain pig on the table and explained, "It's a piggy bank…to keep money in. It was Billy's but now it's yours."

Calvin lifted his eyes from the bank to Verleen. His expression had not changed.

"Ah…I see the problem. You're thinking you have nothing to put in it." She plunked down a handful of money on the table saying, "Now you do."

Calvin just looked at the money and back at her, obviously needing more explanation.

"This is your share of the profits. The egg business has really taken off and now I'm starting to sell milk and butter. You're a big help and have taken on some of the work around here, so now you, me, and Old John are partners." She picked up a few of the coins and started dropping them in the slot located in the pig's back to show him how it was done.

Calvin started sliding the coins into the small opening and she demonstrated how to fold the dollar bills and insert them into the bank also. Once it was all in the bank, he looked at her expectantly.

"Oh, I forgot to show you this," she replied to his unasked question. Turning over the porcelain pig, she removed the rubber plug in the bottom and shook some of the money onto the table. "If you want to spend some of it, this is how you get to it."

Calvin replaced the plug and began depositing the money again.

"You can spend it however you wish. You earned it…and if you want to save it up for something special, that's okay, too. I've got to get back to mopping the floors. Let's hope the rain stops soon. The garden has gotten just what it needs. Too much and all our seeds will wash away and then we'll have to replant." She paused at the doorway leading to the hall and looked back. Calvin had emptied the piggy bank again and was absorbed in dropping the money back through the slot.

The old Chevy truck door groaned as Verleen pulled it open. "Calvin, remind me to oil the hinges on this door when we get back home. This old truck has taken me a many a mile since Elmer and I bought it. I just have to remember to take care of it from time to time and it will take care of me." Grasping the cardboard box that Calvin was holding, she slid it onto the truck seat and then deposited the boy next to it.

"Just a few errands to run today and then maybe we can find a treat on the way home. Think we can do that?" she asked. She didn't really expect a reply and as usual didn't get one.

She drove the truck down the driveway and carefully turned out onto the county road. The truck was uncomfortably warm with the sun glaring through the windshield so she rolled down her window allowing cool air to flow into the cab. It ruffled their hair but kept them from becoming hot and sweaty. *Glad I didn't spend all morning on my hair…not that I ever do. Old Bessie and the chickens could care less what my hair looks like.*

After several minutes, she turned down a lane that led to a farmhouse which sat back off the road much like her own. "Hand me a paper sack from that box," she said climbing out of the truck. With the sack in hand, she approached the porch and climbed the steps. She knocked on the doorframe and peered through the screen door. "Mr. and Mrs. Jenkins?" she called out.

Shuffling footsteps could be heard and then a voice. "Miz Verleen Jackson, how are you this fine morning?" Mr. Jenkins pushed open the screen door. "The missus has the coffee pot on. You come right on in here and have a cup," the elderly man said in greeting.

"I can't stay. I just wanted to come by and bring you some fresh butter I made yesterday and thank you for being such good egg customers. My hens are laying good and I'm selling out fast most days. You call me if you need me to put some back for you. I want to take care of my regular customers," she said kindly.

"We appreciate that, Miz Jackson. You come back when you have time to sit a spell and we thank you for the butter. Hard to come by homemade butter these days." The old man closed the screen door and Verleen watched his stooped frame shuffle toward the back of the house before heading to the truck.

On the road again, Verleen remarked to Calvin, "It's important to check on your neighbors, especially those getting on in age. The Jenkins are good people and tend to keep to themselves. They live off a little social security check they get every month. Never know when they might need something."

They continued on their way, dropping off paper bags holding containers of homemade butter or jelly to Verleen's regular egg customers in the Lolly Springs area. Her last stop was Sally Turner's home, and it was readily apparent that no improvements had been made since their last visit. It looked as run down and neglected as before.

Taking a larger paper sack from the box, she said, "Come on, Calvin. You might want to say hello to Jimmy if he's home." They both climbed out of the truck and went up the steps to the porch. Before they could knock, the front door opened and Jimmy stepped onto the porch looking visibly upset.

"Hi, Nana Vee," he said with no enthusiasm.

"Hey, Jimmy, is your mom home?"

"Yes, ma'am, but she won't come to the door."

"What's wrong, son? Is your momma okay?"

Jimmy just hung his head and looked at his feet.

"Maybe you'd best let me in to take a look at her."

The young man reluctantly took a step back and Verleen and Calvin entered the house. "Sally?" she called gently. She stepped into the kitchen with the little boy following close at her heels. Sally sat at the table holding her sleeping baby. "I baked a ham this week and well…it's just too much for me, Calvin, and Old John to eat all by ourselves. I thought I would bring half for you and the kids…" Her voice trailed off as she rounded the table and got a look at Sally's face.

Chapter 9

Like Jimmy, she wouldn't look directly at Verleen. One eye was swollen closed, surrounded by flesh that was bruised and several red patches on her face were beginning to turn a dark shade of blue.

Verleen inhaled a deep breath and gripped the back of one of the kitchen chairs with white knuckles. Hot anger flooded her system but she tamped it down. This moment called for calm. There had been too much rage already in this house. The young mother's face was evidence of that. "Sally, do you need the doctor?" Verleen asked, working hard to control the emotions she felt.

Sally shook her head. "No, it looks worse than it is," she said in a small, defeated voice.

"No broken bones this time?"

Sally shook her head again.

"Did he hit the kids?"

Sally didn't speak so Jimmy answered for her. "He was coming after Ivy with the belt and I snatched her up and took off outside. Mom jumped in front of the door so he started hittin' on her."

"Where is he now?" Verleen asked through clenched teeth.

"Don't know. Don't care. As long as he's not here," Timmy said angrily from the doorway. Jimmy's twin had stepped into kitchen unnoticed. "He woke up hung over and in a foul mood about noon and left pretty quick. Guess he needed to find another bottle," he bitterly spat out the words.

"Is Ivy alright?" Verleen asked.

"I didn't give him a chance to lay a hand on her." Jimmy's voice was quiet in the still room. "She's napping now in the bedroom."

"I'm sorry, Mom. I wish I'd been here a few minutes earlier. I could have stopped him and I would have…" Timmy's voice choked off as silent tears ran down his face.

Verleen drew another deep breath. She shuddered to think what could have happened and what was likely to happen the next time this occurred.

She set the paper sack on the kitchen counter. In a take-charge manner, Verleen addressed the twins. "Timmy, take the sleeping baby from your momma and put her in the bed with Ivy. They'll both be out for a while and I'll check on them in a bit. I then need both you boys to take Calvin here outside and entertain him while your mom and I have a serious talk."

Timmy wiped his eyes with the back of his hand and then did as Verleen instructed. When he exited the kitchen with the sleeping babe in his arms, Jimmy headed for the front door saying quietly, "Come on, kid, let's go throw the football around."

Calvin looked up at Verleen with big, round eyes, clearly shaken by Timmy's tears and Sally's damaged face. Verleen smiled reassuringly. "It's okay, Calvin. I'll be right here while you play in the yard with the boys. I won't be long. Go on now." She gave him a gentle push and he headed for the front door looking back over his shoulder at her uncertainly.

Verleen waited until she heard Timmy go outside shutting the front door behind him, and in the ensuing silence, she lowered herself into a kitchen chair and rested her crossed arms onto the table. Tears were now flowing down Sally's battered face. She had kept it together until the children were not in the room but there was no holding it back now. Verleen patted her hand and spoke soothing words while she sobbed for several minutes. When the tears slowed, Verleen wet a clean cup towel with cool water and gently wiped Sally's face. She carefully poked and prodded the wounded flesh testing for broken bones as she did so.

"Thanks, Miz Verleen. You always turn up at the right time, don't you?"

"Seems I was later than I should have been, sweetheart," Verleen replied softly.

They sat together in silence for several seconds.

"It's time. Isn't it?" Sally asked looking out the window.

Verleen spoke slowly and deliberately. "It is...the boys are getting big enough to fight that man...and next time when the dust clears, whoever is left standing will go to jail...and the others will be in the hospital...or someplace worse..."

Sally swallowed audibly. "Then, let's do it."

"I think that's the best decision, but just remember...there's no going back or room for second thoughts."

Sally lifted her damaged face and looked straight at the older woman as she said with firm conviction, "Don't worry. I won't be changing my mind."

Verleen nodded in understanding. "It's like we discussed before. I'll send Old John around to your back door with a message. I'll come back by again and check on you in a few days. If Grady comes home drunk again, you call me and get the kids out of here. Run through the woods and meet me at Sawyer's pond."

"I don't think we have to worry about him for the next few days. He usually stays gone for about a week after he…he…" her voice trailed off unwilling to give voice to the violence that had just occurred.

"Alright, then," Verleen patted her hand again. "Feed the kids the ham I brought and call if you need anything. Try to get some rest and I'll see you soon."

Before she reached the front door, she heard Sally let out a long sigh and she hoped it was the sound of a great burden at last being lifted.

Out on the county road once again, Verleen looked down at Calvin in the truck seat beside her. "You okay, little man? I know seeing Sally all beat up like that was scary. Her husband, Grady, is one of those people who has no business drinking alcohol. It changes him and makes him mean as a snake. Did you ever see your folks drink?"

Calvin shook his head.

"Are you sure? Any beer or whiskey at y'all's house?"

This time Calvin shook his head vigorously.

"That's good. You know, one day we're gonna to have to sit down and have a serious talk about your mommy and daddy. You're gonna to have to tell me all about them. If fact, you can start right now. I'm all ears."

Calvin just stared out the windshield as the air rushing through the open window ruffled his brown curls.

Well, maybe his parents didn't get roaring drunk and misplace their kid. I suppose that's one possible explanation we can cross off the list.

"We'll be at Berryville shortly and after we finish our shopping, we'll stop by the Dairy Queen for a burger. Would you like that?"

Calvin nodded enthusiastically and grinned up at her.

"I'm so hungry, I think I could eat….hmmmm, probably 12! How many could you eat?"

Calvin giggled and held up four fingers.

"Is that all? I bet you could eat seven or eight."

Calvin giggled again as they sped down the highway.

Arriving in Berryville, Verleen pulled into a parking spot on Main Street right in front of the Thrif-Tee Market Grocery Store. The market looked busy today and Verleen supposed it was because of the sales that had been advertised in the paper. People moved about the small town going in and out of the businesses that lined the main thoroughfare. Two young ladies leaned up against a parked car nearby talking loudly and waving at people who honked as they passed by. In a town this size, everyone was your friend, neighbor, classmate, part of your church, or part of your family. They honked, waved, and "howdy-eed" when out in public. Of course, that also usually meant everyone knew your business…or thought they did. Small town living had both advantages and drawbacks.

Stopping at the parking meter, Verleen began digging in her purse for change while Calvin waited patiently on the sidewalk beside her. "Well, drat! My wallet was open and all my change got dumped out in the bottom of this big, old purse. Now I'm gonna have to dig." As she fished for nickels to put in the meter, she vaguely overheard the nearby young ladies' conversation. Not that she was eavesdropping but their loud voices carried in their excitement.

"Well, he just kept rolling those dice and winning until he had a big pile of cash sittin' on the table in front of him," the girl in the red dress was saying.

"Did he buy you a cocktail?" asked the girl with glasses.

"Well, several, of course. He said he was winnin' 'cause I was standing there and he had me blow on the dice for good luck."

The girl with glasses responded with elation. "Ooooh, and this was at Boudreaux's Bar on the bayou across the state line? I didn't know they gambled there. I thought it was just drinkin' and dancin'."

Red dress girl's voice dropped a little but it still carried, "Well, they do have this backroom but not just anybody's allowed in there…if you know what I mean."

Glasses girl squealed again and Verleen found the sound very annoying as she continued to fumble around the seemingly bottomless purse. "Hold on a second, Calvin. I've gotta feed the meter some change or risk a parking ticket." Calvin continued to wait placidly as the digging continued.

"Well, are you gonna tell me his name or am I gonna have to drag it out of you?" asked the girl with glasses.

"He said his name was Devon and that he's new around here. He asked me if I was there every Friday night," the red dress girl gushed enthusiastically. "In fact, I think that's his car coming down the street now. Don't look! Don't look! Wait till he passes!"

As the shiny, black car slid slowly past, the driver tapped the horn and the red dress girl feigned surprise and flashed a big smile and a wave. Both girls stared after the car and then squealed in excitement as it turned the corner.

They weren't the only ones staring down the street…so was Verleen who thought she caught a glimpse of a hawkish profile behind the wheel.

Chapter 10

Verleen inserted a couple of coins in the parking meter and turned the crank. "There, that ought to do it." Taking Calvin by the hand, she headed for the front of the store, but instead of going inside, she walked down to the corner of the building where a pay phone was mounted. She parked Calvin on a wooden bench conveniently located a few feet away. The wood shavings on the ground attested to the fact that it was the local whittlers' bench, and lucky for Verleen, it was empty today. The old men who usually occupied it with their carving knives and world-problem-solving discussions were elsewhere at the moment. Looking about, she felt satisfied that she was far enough from the front door so that no one could overhear her conversation; she dropped in the necessary change and dialed the number she had committed to memory.

While she spoke at length, she kept her eye on Calvin who sat on the bench swinging his feet. When he grew restless, he pulled a small, toy car out of his pocket and began to run it up and down the wooden bench slats making quiet motor noises to himself.

Once her business was concluded, Verleen hung up the phone and called to Calvin. "Let's go, sweetie. I promise we just have this one quick, last thing to do and then it's burger time!"

True to her word, the grocery shopping was done in a flash. With their purchases stowed in the floorboard, they pulled the old truck into the Dairy Queen parking lot. At the counter, Verleen placed their order and they had their pick of tables because they were the only customers in the place. Sliding into seats, Calvin looked around in wonder at the plate glass windows, the red booths, and the various posters of frozen ice cream treats on the wall.

"Did your mommy and daddy ever take you to a Dairy Queen before?" Verleen asked.

Calvin shook his head.

"What about that grocery store we just left? Have you ever been to it?"

Calvin shook his head once again.

"What about Berryville? Do you think you've ever been to this town?"

This time Calvin just shrugged slightly as if to say, "I haven't the foggiest."

Verleen sighed. "You know, all this chattering you do all day long is just making my ears feel like they are gonna fall off."

One side of Calvin's mouth went up in a little half smile.

"Here y'all go…two burgers, an order of fries, and two cokes." The waitress in the smock set down the red plastic tray and walked away and they wasted no time in diving into their food. Calvin must have been as hungry as Verleen because he ate every bite of his kid burger and half of the fries they shared.

"I guess we have the chickens to thank for these burgers. The egg business is booming and people are coming from all around to buy us out. Come to think of it, they started laying eggs like crazy about the time you came to stay. Have you been sweet talkin' those hens? Well, whatever you're doing, keep doing it." She winked at Calvin and smiled. "I think we should celebrate our new business success with a special treat. How 'bout a Dilly Bar?"

Calvin just tilted his head and raised his eyebrows.

"A Dilly Bar…don't tell me you've never had one. It's frozen ice cream on a stick and it's covered in chocolate."

Calvin still looked lost.

Verleen glanced around for help. "There." She pointed at the shiny poster on the wall. "One of those."

Calvin took one look at the poster and his eyes lit up.

Seriously…this kid has never had a Dilly Bar? Every kid in Texas has had one before they can walk!

Verleen said, "You just have to do me one teensy, tiny favor. You just have to say, 'Dilly Bar'."

Calvin looked at Verleen and then back at the poster.

"Come on…just those two magic words…I want to hear 'em." Verleen cupped her hand behind one ear and leaned forward across the table.

Calvin gazed at the poster and then back at Verleen once again in reluctance. Dropping his eyes to the table and ducking his head, he whispered, "Dilly Bar."

"That's the ticket!" Verleen said slapping the table enthusiastically. She propelled herself out of her seat in a heartbeat, sliding the required money across the counter saying, "One Dilly Bar, please." In the booth once again, she pulled the plastic wrap off of the ice cream and presented it to Calvin with glee.

While Calvin was absorbed in devouring his ice cream, Verleen sat and sipped the rest of her coke in satisfaction. *Ahhh, the magic of ice cream...it has power to soothe the savage beast...and to compel the mute to speak.*

A few days later, Verleen and Calvin sped down the county road again in the old truck. This time their outing was one of a different nature. Verleen turned off the county road onto a dirt road, and they drove several miles back into the woods before she rolled the old truck to a stop under the shade of a big oak tree. "This is it. Let's get our gear out of the back of the truck and see what kind of luck we have today."

Reaching into the bed of the vehicle, she handed cane fishing poles to Calvin and grabbed the tackle box and buckets to carry herself. "Mind those hooks now. Don't want to have one of those snag you." They hauled the gear a few yards away to the edge of the river and she selected a nice, cool, shady place for them to set up. Once they were sitting on the overturned buckets, Verleen baited their hooks with worms and showed Calvin how to drop his line in the water. "Now we wait for a hungry catfish to come along and bite on that tasty worm. When you see that cork go under and feel a tug on your line, pull it up. Keep a tight grip on your pole or Old Mr. Catfish will pull it right out of your hands and swim off with it."

Calvin nodded in understanding and Verleen kept watch out of the corner of her eye for any slackness in his grip. A perfect day for fishing, the slow flow of the muddy water sliding by just put one in a state of relaxation. "Your folks ever take you fishing?"

Calvin shook his head.

Of course not...seems as though this kid has never lived any sort of life until now. The sudden wave of animosity she felt toward his parents caught her by surprise. *Did they just birth him and put him in a closet?*

"Ever hear of the Neches River?"

She didn't even have to look in his direction to know that he shook his head.

"This here's the Neches River and all the woods around here are what is known as the Big Thicket. It's not as big as it used to be. Civilization has been nibbling at its edges for years now but it still covers thousands of acres. Lots of wild animals live in that big forest. The logging companies are cutting it down as fast as they can. If somebody doesn't do something soon, all the critters will have nowhere to go. I guess when that happens, they'll all just disappear." Verleen's voice was sad at the prospect of the wild, ancient forest and its inhabitants slowly fading away.

She doubted the little boy understood all of what she was saying but she continued anyway. She sighed heavily, "I guess there's just no stopping progress. See that white cloud of smoke to the south just above the trees? That's a factory several miles away and this river runs pretty close to it. It opened about 16 years ago and while it has created lots of jobs for people who were struggling, it hasn't been good for this river. Everybody knows that they dump pollution into the water when no one's looking. The locals have filed complaints but nobody does anything about it. Besides, if you protest too loudly, your family or friends find themselves unemployed. Just remember to always fish north of the factory. You don't want to be eatin' any fish caught downstream of it."

Just about that moment, Calvin jumped up from his bucket and raised his pole as high as his little arms could but his hook didn't quite clear the water. Verleen could see something thrashing under the surface. "That's right…hold on…don't let it get away!" She grabbed the dip net and scooped up the wriggling fish that was trying its best to throw the hook. It was a nice size catfish and just perfect for frying up in a skillet.

Removing the hook from its mouth, she dropped the fish into the wire basket that was lowered into the edge of the water. She quickly re-baited Calvin's hook and he lost no time in plopping it into the river. "You sure you haven't ever been fishing before? You handle that fishing pole just like a pro!"

Calvin beamed up at her and then turned his concentration back to the cork floating on the river current. Verleen pick up her pole from the river bank and resumed her seat on her bucket. "See how the roots of that cypress tree reach into the river? I bet there's a bunch of catfish hiding there close to the bank."

A small boat carrying two men slowly putted by in midstream heading up river, and the men waved in a friendly manner as they passed. As the motor's noise faded into the distance, a sparrow settled in the branches overhead and began a lovely song as a cool spring breeze continued to move along the river. Verleen felt her eyelids grow heavy and her chin had just about dipped to rest on her chest when she felt something tug at her own line. Snapping to attention, she lifted her own pole out of the water and pulled in a fish of medium size. "We keep this up and we're gonna have us a fish fry! Check your hook, Calvin, and make sure the fish haven't nibbled that worm off."

Calvin did so and plunked his still-baited hook back into the water. Two seconds later he was making excited noises and pulling his pole up with all his might. The end of his cane pole bent down in an arc toward the water with what had to be a huge fish on the line!

Chapter 11

"Verleen?" Gracie's voice came from the front porch.

"Come on in, Gracie. I'm in the kitchen," Verleen yelled back.

Gracie came through the living room and deposited a bowl of green salad on the already-set kitchen table. "Mmmm…that sure does smell good!"

"We're gonna be ready to eat in two shakes of a fat lamb's tail," Verleen said adding a large platter of fried catfish to the table that already held plates of hush puppies, fried potatoes, and a bowl of pinto beans. "Grab the ketchup and tartar sauce out of fridge and I'll open a jar of pickled green tomatoes. There…I think that's everything. Let me call the boys in."

Sticking her head around the screen door, she announced, "Get on in here, you two. Supper's on the table."

Calvin and Old John rose from the back steps where they had been relaxing and made haste into the kitchen. Everyone took their places at the table and a prayer of thanks was promptly offered. For the next few minutes, the kitchen was filled only with the sound of plates being passed and the clinking of utensils.

Gracie was the first to speak, "Calvin, I do declare that you must have caught the tastiest catfish in the entire river!"

"Too bad Earl couldn't join us," Verleen interjected. Gracie's husband worked out of town and was away from home often.

Old John bobbed his head in agreement, "This is some good eatin', boy. Miz Vee, you outdid yo'self with the fish."

"We had us a time on the river yesterday and came home with a good mess of fish. Didn't we, Calvin?"

Calvin looked up from his plate and grinned around the mouthful of food that he had tucked away in each cheek like a chipmunk. The mouthwatering strips of cornmeal-coated, deep-fried catfish were quickly disappearing from his plate and everyone else's.

"Save room for cake, everybody," Verleen remarked as she got up to refill their tea glasses.

"Lemon?" Gracie asked hopefully.

"Of course, lemon…dare I make anything else? I'm afraid you'd turn your nose up at some other kind of cake."

Gracie just snickered and Old John smiled at the two best friends' affable banter. "Calvin, how many fish did you catch yesterday?" Gracie asked.

Calvin put down his fork and held up nine fingers.

"And how many did Nana Vee catch?"

Calvin cast a sidelong glance at Verleen as he slowly held up one finger and everyone burst out laughing.

"Vee, I thought you said you caught half these fish!" Gracie teased.

Verleen was quick to reply, "Gracie, I did not and you know it."

"Guess I better get my hearing checked. Calvin, don't let Nana Vee take any credit for your catches. What size was the biggest one you caught?"

Calvin held his hands about 18 inches apart.

"And how big was the **one** Nana Vee caught?"

Calvin's hands slowly came up and spread apart about nine inches and then just as slowly came closer together to stop at a position indicating five inches.

The entire table erupted in loud laughter once again and supper was consumed with more good-natured ribbing and jokes at Verleen's expense.

Later the two ladies stood at the sink while Verleen washed the dishes and Gracie rinsed. They both watched out the kitchen window as the little boy and the old man took turns throwing the tennis ball against the shed wall.

"That fish was delicious, Vee. I can't remember the last time I had fried catfish. I think I ate too much," said Gracie.

"We all did. None of us had room for dessert. I'll have to send some cake home with everybody to eat later."

"Did you see how much Calvin put away? Is his appetite that good all the time?"

"Yep, pretty much has been from day one. He can hold his own at the table."

"I wonder why the little fellow hasn't grown any?"

"What do you mean?"

"Well, when kids tuck into a full plate like he just did, it usually means they're fixin' to go through a growing spurt."

"He's growing…just look at him…I mean…he is growing. Isn't he?" Verleen sounded uncertain.

Gracie shook her head. "Henry's clothes fit him just like they did on the day I brought them over. He's exactly the same size. In fact, don't send them back 'cause Henry's outgrown them now." She paused for a second and continued apologetically. "I didn't mean to worry you. I just thought it was odd. Probably you'll look up one day and them jeans will be too short. Some kids do that. They save all their growing for one big sprout up."

Verleen was slow to respond, "Yeah, I bet that's what is gonna happen. Guess I just hadn't noticed. It's been a long time since I've had a little boy around here. Billy's been gone for so long," she answered quietly.

Their conversation fell silent for several minutes as they both realized they had strayed off into painful memories for Verleen.

She gave her friend a little smile and said confidently, "I suspect any day now those jeans and T-shirts will start lookin' too short and we'll be headin' over to Birdwell's in Berryville to get him some new ones."

"I'm sure you're right, Vee," Gracie replied quickly to soothe her friend's uneasiness. "You suppose that little boy is ever gonna start talking? I mean, he didn't say two words the entire time at the supper table," Gracie complained.

"Well, actually he said quite a bit with you egging him on," Verleen replied dryly.

Gracie snickered. "You're usually quite the fisherman, Vee. How in the world did that little feller out fish you?"

Verleen's hands paused in the soapy water as she stared out the window. "You know…it was the oddest thing. It was as if those fish were lined up and taking turns jumping on his hook. One time I don't think I even had the chance to put the worm on his hook, and he dropped it down in the water only to pull it right back up with a catfish on it. Never saw anything like it…" She shook herself out of her reverie and resumed scrubbing. "And he did say two words the other day."

"What?"

"I said, 'He did say two words the other day'."

"I heard you…I meant what two words did he say?"

"Dilly Bar."

"DILLY BAR? The boy doesn't talk for weeks and when he finally opens his mouth he says, 'Dilly Bar'? Of all the crazy things for him land on…" Gracie sputtered.

"Well…we **were** sittin' at the Dairy Queen in Berryville." Verleen was enjoying her friend's perplexity.

"You know, Vee…you could have led with that," Gracie said in exasperation.

"Yeah, I could have but what fun would that be?"

Gracie rolled her eyes. "Vee, I swear you have the devil in you."

"I'm sure that's what folks around here say about me," her voice dripped with sarcasm.

Gracie was quiet for several seconds. "That's not exactly what they say…" she said rather lamely.

Verleen glanced at her friend. "When did I ever give a hoot about what people say about me?" she said with a slight chuckle.

"You really did give folks something to gossip about when you threw those eggs on the floor in Pete Miller's Mercantile."

"I'll have you know I **dropped** those eggs accidentally," she replied with pronounced indignance.

"Sure you did," Gracie shot back jeeringly.

They both snickered at that.

"Of course, a few people aren't comfortable about you feeding an old, black man at your table."

"I don't really care," Verleen replied derisively.

"I know, Vee. I know. They're really all a bunch of meddling busybodies who have nothing better to do than to sit around tending to everyone else's business." She paused and then added in an offhand sort of manner, "Of course, your lack of church-going also rubs some people the wrong way."

Verleen burst out laughing at the last remark. "So this is where the gossip is coming from? The members of your church listen to sermons on Sunday and then spread rumors about me in Sunday school… or do they wait 'til they're on the front lawn afterwards …talk about hypocrites…" She howled with laughter again.

To Gracie's credit, she did turn a little pink. "Vee, you know I don't gossip about you. It's just that I overheard some talking and I thought you should know…"

When Verleen could get control of herself, she used the cup towel by the sink to wipe her wet eyes. "You know, Gracie, maybe I need to hear some of this talk myself. If I can scrounge up a dress around here somewhere, I may just put it on and show up next Sunday morning and sit on the front row. Better yet, I'll drag Old John with me. We'll get there early and sit in the Widow Comeaux's pew. That will have tongues wagging and the party lines will be buzzing all over town."

Gracie shook her head and almost rolled her eyes clean out of her head. "Vee, you take the cake…you really do…" she said in resignation.

"Cake? Are we having dinner on the ground after preaching? I'll bring a cake!" she said with exaggerated excitement.

"It's a good thing that I know you're truly a good Christian woman or I would really worry about you," Gracie said with a sigh.

Still snickering, Verleen was barely choked out her next words, "And in honor of the Widow Comeaux…I'll make it lemon!"

"Whatever floats your moat, Vee," Gracie said under her breath, clearly not amused…but Verleen was amused, and she plopped onto a kitchen chair as fresh gales of laughter erupted leaving her breathless.

Chapter 12

Verleen sat on the back porch sewing patches on a pair of Calvin's jeans of which he had worn the knees clear through. She kept an eye on two little boys playing happily in the yard. Gracie had dropped off little Henry earlier in the morning right after breakfast, and the two had taken to each other right off the bat. They had bounced the tennis ball off the shed wall, and growing tired of that, they had played in the dirt with Calvin's truck and tractor collection. At the moment, they pushed each other on the tire swing having a grand time as evidenced by their whoops and hollers. Verleen could hear a steady stream of talking coming from little Henry and sometimes she thought she could just barely make out replies from Calvin.

The two boys approached the porch at a run and collapsed out of breath onto the wooden steps. They were hot and sweaty and barefoot since the day was warm enough to go without shoes.

"Nana Vee, can we have some Kool-Aid? We're thirsty," asked Henry.

"You sure can. I'll make a pitcher right now. What flavor do you want? I have grape, strawberry, and cherry," she answered.

The two boys looked at each other and then Henry said, "We both want strawberry."

Verleen asked, "How do you know what Calvin wants?"

"He tolded me," Henry said matter-of-factly.

Calvin nodded in agreement and Verleen returned shortly with plastic glasses filled with ice and Kool-Aid. After quickly downing their drinks, the boys jumped up and raced around the yard in an impromptu game of chase. Verleen returned to her pants patching and shook her head. She couldn't quite make out the rules of the game but the boys were having a good time with nary a cross word between them.

"Hey, Boone, why are you up here on the porch? You should be out in the yard with the boys." Hearing his name, the dog lifted his head and looked around, yawned and resumed his napping position. "Yep, they have way too much energy for me, too. Neither one of us could keep up with them. I guess us old dogs should just stay on the porch."

Later, Verleen noticed the boys standing on the edge of the garden. They knew better than to chase each other through the plowed area and had carefully skirted it in their game of chase. Henry was apparently asking questions and Calvin seemed to be answering and pointing out various parts of the garden. When Calvin satisfied Henry's curiosity about the garden, they took off running again and flitted about the yard like dragonflies, stopping here and there for a few seconds and then dashing off again. The next time Verleen glanced their way, they were hanging upside down from a low limb of a tree on the edge of the yard. Verleen chuckled and shook her head. *Typical boys...full of motion and mayhem.*

Gracie showed up at lunch time and they ate sandwiches on the porch for their midday meal. "Have you boys had a good time?" she asked.

Both boys responded with nods of their heads since their mouths were stuffed with baloney sandwiches being washed down with more strawberry Kool-Aid.

"I hope Henry has been behaving himself," Gracie said to Verleen.

"Henry always behaves when he comes over to Nana Vee's house," she replied fondly and winked at Henry who flashed a smile back from his seat on the top step.

"I have some cookies for y'all to take home when you go," Verleen informed Gracie.

"You know I can't take sweets to my house with my diabetical husband home from work," Gracie retorted.

"Well, I was sending them home for Henry and I don't think diabetical is a real word, Gracie."

"I'm pretty sure it is, Miz Know-It-All," Gracie shot back as she reached for a cookie from the plate sitting on the table between the rockers.

"Diabolical or diabetic? Pick one," Verleen explained with exaggerated patience.

"So I just saved time by using two words instead of one...excuse me, professor," she replied sarcastically and then continued, "It just means he has a raging appetite for sweets so don't send no cookies home. He'll just find them and eat them all or Henry will and next thing you know I'll have two diabeticals on my hands," Gracie concluded matter-of-factly.

"Your ability to butcher the English language never ceases to amaze me," Verleen said under her breath.

In answer, Gracie picked up another cookie and bit into it rather deliberately. "I'll eat a few extra to save them from themselves, 'cause I'm just considerate that way."

Verleen snickered at her comical friend. *Never a dull moment when Gracie is around. That's for sure.*

Little Henry chose that moment to speak up, "I sure hope I can come back when the watermelons git ripe. Calvin said y'all planted a bunch of them and he said he never hadded watermelon before. I told him he would love it and he asked if it tastes better than peas, and I told him it tastes a **lot** better than peas and beans and corn and okra…and anythang in that garden…"

"He said all that?" Gracie asked in surprise. She and Verleen passed a look between them.

"Calvin, why don't you give Miz Gracie a tour of the garden?" Verleen suggested.

Calvin popped the last bite of sandwich into his mouth, took Gracie by the hand, and they strolled across the yard together.

Verleen made her voice as nonchalant as possible, "Henry, does Calvin only talk to you when there's no one else around?"

Henry shook his head and bit into his second baloney sandwich. "He walks oil da ime."

"What did you say?"

Henry took a moment to chew and swallow. "He talks all the time. Can I have one of those cookies?"

"Sure, kiddo. You might want to finish that sandwich first."

Moving to the top step to sit beside Henry, she watched as he polished off the sandwich and then handed him a cookie.

Gracie and Calvin returned to the porch and when lunch was over, their visitors took their leave with Gracie promising to bring her grandson back another time so the two could play again.

Verleen rocked in her chair a few minutes and then quietly asked, "So you've never had watermelon before, Calvin?"

Calvin shook his head.

"What fruits have you ever eaten? Do you remember?"

Calvin shook his head again and continued to chomp on his cookie from his place on the steps and looked out across the yard.

He's a chatterbox with Henry but clams up around adults. Verleen sighed. *I guess it's gonna take more time before he feels safe enough to talk to me.*

Later at suppertime, Calvin barely made it through his fried chicken. His eyes kept closing as he chewed and his head dipped toward his plate a few times. *All that fresh air and sunshine and running around in the yard has him tuckered out.* "Come on, Calvin, you're gonna go face down in your pie if you sit there much longer."

Scooping him up from his chair, she carried him toward his bedroom. With his head on her shoulder, she heard him whisper, "Want to eat pie…"

Verleen chuckled. *Who doesn't like pie?* "I'll save it for you and you can have it for breakfast in the morning." She breathed in deeply of his freshly-bathed scent as she slid him under the covers. Kissing him on the forehead, she tucked the covers in around him and smoothed his hair back. She made sure the nightlight was on and paused at the door and looked back. Whispering in the semi-dark, she said, "I love you, Calvin…sweet dreams." Leaving the door cracked, she returned to the kitchen and began putting away the supper leftovers. It took her a few minutes to realize that he had finally spoken without being prompted and she stopped in her tracks in surprise. *Well, what do you know? I'll bake a pie every day if that's what it takes!*

Hours later, Verleen sat at the kitchen table still wearing her day clothes. Glancing at the clock, she noted it was nearing one in the morning. She had dozed on the couch after cleaning up the kitchen and then at midnight had brewed a fresh pot of coffee and was enjoying her second cup. She had checked on Calvin several times, but he was in deep slumber and slept undisturbed. She picked up a pencil and returned to the crossword puzzle that she had been working on. There was always one in the Sunday newspaper so she kept the section folded to the puzzle on the kitchen table and would write in an answer or two as they occurred to her during the week. It didn't matter that she usually didn't complete the entire puzzle before the next Sunday rolled around.

At this age, it's all about keeping your mind sharp. Let's see…a four-letter word meaning storm. Hmmmm….GALE…yep that fits. She scribbled in the answer. *Starting with 'L' meaning sluggish…LANGUID…drat…that doesn't work. I'll have to come back to that one. Next word starts with an 'E'…has 16 letters and means unearthly---*

Verleen's thoughts were interrupted by Boone setting up a howl on the back porch. Dropping the newspaper and rising quickly from the table, she hustled to the door and as she opened it, a tall figure stepped out of the darkness of the yard and stood at the foot of the steps. Even though the porch light shone, it cast a weak light that did not reach the

man's features which were hidden in the shadow cast by the brim of his
hat.

Chapter 13

Boone stopped barking the minute Verleen stepped out onto the porch. Seeing that she was aware of the intruder, he flopped back down onto his usual sleeping spot on the wooden floor to resume his rest.

The strange figure was quiet for a moment and then said softly, "Miss Jackson, I hope I didn't wake all the neighbors."

"You come right on in, Brother Goodman. No one's gonna pay much attention to a dog barking and I don't have any neighbors close by anyway. You find my place with no problem?"

The man climbed the steps and came into the kitchen following Verleen. "It's been a while since I've been here and I made a few wrong turns, but I eventually found my way. Not many markers and signs out here on the country backroads."

Verleen motioned the man into a chair at the table and set a cup of coffee in front of him. He placed his hat in a nearby chair revealing dark hair encroached by grey. He wore a black suit and tie and his face, though starting to age, wore a kind expression. He helped himself to the cream and sugar on the table and Verleen followed the coffee with a plate holding a slice of cake.

"I hope this is that prize-winning lemon cake I've heard about, Miz Jackson."

Verleen looked surprised. "How did you know about that?"

He chuckled as he took a bite, "Well, we do have our sources, you know...it's important for us to keep tabs on our...ummm...helpers...and we discovered a while back that you were quite the baker."

Verleen chuckled softly and shook her head in amazement as she took a sip of coffee.

The man continued, "I do believe this is the best cake I've ever had, and I will be passing on that information...along with other things."

Before she could respond, a soft voice called from the other side of the screen door. "Nana Vee, it's Jimmy."

Verleen opened the screen door for the young man. "Everybody with you, son?"

"Yes, ma'am. They's hanging back 'til I checked it out." Turning away from the door, he nodded toward the yard, and Sally and all of her clan came out of the gloom and entered the kitchen.

The two little ones were fast asleep, the baby in Sally's arms, and Ivy was being held by Timmy with her head on his shoulder. Jimmy carried a suitcase in his hand and had various tote bags slung over his shoulders.

Verleen made introductions all around and had everyone sit at the table. The babies never stirred and slept on unaware and everyone spoke softly so that they would continue to sleep.

The tall man cleared his throat and addressed Sally. "Did you have any trouble getting out of the house tonight, Mrs. Turner?"

Sally shook her head. "I kept the kids out of his way so as not to set him off and then when he was…." She swallowed and looked away in embarrassment, "…drunk and passed out, we snuck out. After he ties on a good one, he don't wake up 'til late the next day."

Sally looked tired and drained and her face still showed the trace of bruises that had just begun to fade.

"Well, then…any questions?"

Sally shook her head.

"Any second thoughts? There won't be a return trip once we take this step. I must make sure you understand that."

Sally looked at the man and didn't blink. "I'm never coming back to this town. I want better than this for my children and I'm gonna do whatever it takes," she said with determination.

Verleen let out her breath in relief. "Good, good…that's good. This is going to make things easier. How are you boys feeling about all this?" she asked looking at the twins.

"Nothing around here I'm gonna miss," Jimmy said with a trace of bitterness and Timmy nodded his agreement.

"You boys continue to be a blessing to your momma. Do what Brother Goodman tells you. Him and his people are going to give you a new life a long ways away from here," Verleen said.

Someone across the kitchen let out a long yawn and Verleen turned to find Calvin standing in the entrance to the hallway rubbing his eyes. He padded across the kitchen and leaned against Verleen's side blinking his eyes blearily at the crowd around the table. Verleen slipped her arm around him. "We didn't mean to wake you up, sugar. Go back to bed." Calvin headed back toward the hallway but stopped unnoticed at the edge of the kitchen.

Verleen rose and opened the refrigerator. Handing two large paper sacks to Brother Goodman she said, "I know y'all have a long trip ahead of you so I packed some cold fried chicken, cookies, and other snacks to help y'all along your way. These kids are gonna be hungry come daylight."

As the family began to gather their things to take their leave, Sally saw Verleen hand Brother Goodman some folded cash. She began to protest immediately. "You've done enough for us already. The food and… helping us get away from here---"

The man holding the bags of food spoke softly, "Mrs. Tucker, Verleen here contributes regularly to our mission of providing safe haven for families in trouble. Yours is not the only family we've relocated in the middle of the night."

Understanding gradually dawned on Sally's face and she looked back and forth from the man to Verleen. Speaking slowly she said, "You and your…people…have done this before?"

"Yes, ma'am, this has all been planned out ahead of time. Don't worry about the details," the man replied.

"Is your name really Goodman?"

The man smiled gently, "It's best not to know real names when we do this. Makes it a lot harder for anyone to follow your trail. When I get your family to where we're going, you will be placed in safe hands and you won't ever see me again. There are Christian people waiting to help you begin a new life with a place to live, new schools for the kids, and new names so that Grady can never find you and hurt you ever again."

With tears streaming down her face, Sally hugged Verleen as best she could with the baby in her arms between them. "I'm never gonna see you again, am I?" she whispered.

Verleen said, "It's to keep you safe. We've discussed this already. No phone calls or letters. Those can lead to anyone finding you…even the authorities. We both know if Grady ever found you, he'd probably kill you…and hurt these kids. These are good people, Sally…trust them. We can only hope that in time the kids will forget all the bad things that happened in that house."

"But how can I ever repay you for taking care of me and my kids so many times?"

"Oh, honey, you can repay me by going out that door without looking back and getting you a real life, and when you get the chance to help someone else, you do that."

Sally drew back and looked Verleen in the face for a long moment and then she said in a resolute voice, "Come on, boys…it's time."

Brother Goodman was holding the screen door open as the family began to file out. Before Sally could step out the door, a small hand tugged at her skirt tail. Looking down, she was surprised to see Calvin reaching up to hand her wad of cash.

Confused, Sally glanced at Verleen. "Oh, no, sweetie…"

Calvin gestured again with the money, wanting her to take it.

Verleen had to clear her throat before she could speak, "It's the money from his piggy bank. I told him he could spend it or save it for something important. I guess the little feller figures this is something important."

Calvin tucked the money in Sally's dress pocket and then went to Verleen's side. The young mother looked out into the night where her family had disappeared and then ducked her head to stare at the floor at her feet. Without looking back, she stepped out onto the porch and her words came floating back from darkness.

"I'm gonna miss you, Miz Verleen. Maybe my life would have been better if I'd had a momma like you. I won't ever forget you and Calvin and everything you've done for me." And then she was gone.

Verleen stepped to the screen door and peered out seeing nothing. A few moments later, she heard a car engine start in the distance and for the second time tonight breathed a long sigh of relief. "Lord, take care of Sally and those babies. I've done all I can. They're in your hands now," she prayed softly.

Swiping at the tears that had gathered at the corner of her eyes, she turned to the sleepy child who swayed on his feet. Scooping him up, she headed down the hall to tuck him once more into bed.

Chapter 14

"The garden is coming along nicely," Verleen said as she paused to look back at the work that had taken all afternoon. She had stopped and leaned on her hoe to take a break. She glanced at Old John and Calvin but could barely make out their features that were hidden in shadow cast by the straw hats they all wore. The Texas sun could be fierce on cloudless days such as this one, and even someone as dark-skinned as Verleen could get a painful burn making long sleeves and hats necessary. Verleen's leathered complexion reflected years of working outside and was due, in part, to her Cherokee heritage on her father's side of the family.

Unfortunately, her paternal Native American grandmother died before Verleen was born, and she had inherited the brown skin genetics but none of the culture to go along with it.

Old John, Verleen, and Calvin spent hours uprooting the beginnings of weeds that popped up in the plowed soil and would overtake the growing space if left unattended. Using their hoes and rakes carefully, they loosened the dirt and gently pulled it up to the stems of the small seedlings that were beginning to make their way to the surface. "Can't wait to eat some of these new potatoes when they're ready. I can just taste a fried tater sandwich right now," Verleen said wistfully.

Old John grunted in agreement.

Calvin had stopped pulling weeds to stare up at Verleen in puzzlement.

"Now don't tell me you've never eaten a fried tater sandwich."

Calvin shook his head.

"Where in the world have you been?" she asked in wonderment. "I see I have my work cut out for me. As soon as the potatoes are ready to dig, we gonna fry some up and I'll introduce you to a southern delicacy!"

Calvin smiled in response.

That boy does love his groceries. I haven't found much he won't eat. Of course, there was that time I tried to feed him liver, but it's an acquired taste…so I guess that doesn't count.

Reaching the end of the last row, they all turned back to look in satisfaction at what they had accomplished. Verleen said, "I guess we have done all we can in the garden for the time being. Let's go cool off on the porch."

They put the garden tools away and trudged up to the steps. Verleen disappeared into the kitchen and returned with glasses of iced tea and they sat in the porch rockers and sipped. They had all worked up a light sweat in the bright sun and the cold tea hit the spot.

"Calvin, my flower bed here by the porch is looking a mite thirsty. Grab that water hose and give it a little drink for me."

As the boy hopped up and did as Verleen instructed, Old John and Verleen began chatting about when to plant the tomatoes or rather Verleen chatted and Old John just nodded, as was his way. A few sprinkles from the garden hose reached Verleen's outstretched feet so she pulled them back from the edge of the porch and resumed her rocking. A few minutes later, her knees received a few drops from the watering the flowerbed was receiving, and  she glanced at Calvin to make sure he knew where he was aiming the water. He appeared to be intent on his assigned task so she turned back to her one-sided conversation with Old John. Several minutes passed and then she felt a generous amount of water hit her lap and looking back over in Calvin's direction once again, she caught a glimpse of a slight smile that he was attempting to hide.

"You little rascal! I told you to water the flowers, not me!"

Calvin broke into a broad smile and slowly started shifting the stream of water her way.

Verleen jumped up from her rocker and headed down the steps and that's when the cold water hit her full force. Squealing and laughing, she headed for Calvin who was running backwards with the hose and squirting her the entire time. She tried to dodge the water but had no luck and was drenched immediately. Reaching him, she wrestled the water hose away and turned it on him. He collapsed on the ground laughing.

Calvin finally gained his footing and started running away from the steady flow of water that she aimed at the back of his head. He jumped behind the trunk of a nearby tree and peeked around it while Verleen shot at any part of him that appeared within her sight.

Dashing across the yard once more, Calvin reached the unguarded faucet and quickly turned it off. Dripping water and looking like two drowned rats, they both had trouble standing as they weakened from uncontrollable laughing. The sound of Old John's cackles of amusement reached them from the porch. Verleen held up her hands and waved them back and forth. "Truce! Truce! I call a truce!"

Dragging the water hose toward the side of the house where the faucet was located, she said, "Let me wind up this hose and then we'll go in and get cleaned up." Calvin was heading toward the steps when the water struck him in the back. Verleen had turned on the water once again upon reaching its source. The water fight immediately resumed and went on for some time with Old John slapping his knees and roaring with laughter through it all. The skirmish finally ended when Verleen dashed into the house hollering, "I give! I give!" Shouting out the kitchen window, she said, "I'm gonna put on some dry clothes and heat us up some supper."

Minutes later, she sat at the kitchen table with Old John while leftover chicken and rice heated in the oven and Calvin soaked in the bathtub.

"'Mind me not to turn my back when one of y'all has that water hose in hand," Old John chuckled.

Verleen laughed. "That boy is a mess, for sure!"

"You's both a mess, Miz Vee."

"Everybody needs to act like a kid now and then, I reckon. Besides…that cold water did feel good after working up a sweat. Anytime you feel too warm this summer in the garden, you just say the word. Calvin or I will be happy to cool you off," she remarked helpfully.

"I'm sho' y'all would," he replied with a chuckle.

Later when the supper dishes were done and Old John had taken his leftovers and headed for home, Verleen joined Calvin in the living room. The national news was on and the young boy was once again glued to the television. During commercials, he laid on the floor with the newspaper spread out and stared at it, turning pages now and then.

Don't know what he finds so fascinating. There aren't that many pictures in it and very few comics. The next time I'm in Berryville, I'll pick up some children's books at the Five-and-Dime Store and we'll start reading a book every night at bedtime.

Verleen propped her feet up on the ottoman and resumed her latest knitting project. Gracie had yet another grandbaby on the way and she was working on a pair of yellow baby booties as a gift.

When the news went off, Calvin flipped channels for several minutes and seemed to be bored with the choice of television programs. "Come sit by me a minute, little man," said Verleen patting the couch beside her.

Dutifully, Calvin climbed up onto the couch and sat silently watching her slide the yellow yarn across the needles. "You really didn't have to give Sally all the money from your piggy bank, sweetie...but I really appreciate that you did. It shows you have a generous spirit." She slipped an arm around the small boy and gave him a tight squeeze. "You know...life here on earth is just harder for some people. I was lucky to have my sweet husband, Elmer, but Sally and her kids had it really rough for a long time. She and the kids are in good hands now and their lives are already better, but we can't tell anyone about their leaving. You do understand, don't you? To keep them safe, we have to keep it a secret."

Calvin gazed up at her with his big, brown eyes and nodded. *I really do think he understands...maybe he's seen some rough stuff in his own family...who knows?* "The way those chickens are laying, we'll have your piggy bank filled up again in no time. And the next time we go to Berryville, Nana Vee is buying you two Dilly Bars at the Dairy Queen for being such sweet boy."

Calvin grinned and rubbed his belly in anticipation. They watched some silly show for a while in comfortable silence. "Change the channel, Calvin. I think it's about time for *The Waltons*. That's one of the few good TV shows on these days."

The boy crossed to the television and flipped the knob until he landed on the correct station and the familiar theme music swelled into the room. For the next hour, the two companions lived life during the Great Depression in the mountains of Virginia with John Walton and his brood of seven children. When the show came to a satisfying end with all of the characters' problems successfully handled, Verleen herded Calvin off to bed. The sleepy, little boy climbed into bed with a loud yawn and settled under the covers. She smoothed the hair from his forehead and there placed a light kiss as that had become their nightly ritual. As she passed through the door and flipped off the light switch, she thought she heard a voice whisper in the semi-darkness, "Goodnight, John-Boy."

Chapter 15

Verleen and Calvin stood on the front porch with brooms, buckets, and various other cleaning supplies. After knocking spider webs down from the corners and washing the windows, the rocking chairs, outside house walls, and porch floor sparkled from a good scrubbing. Spring in Southeast Texas was porch-sittin' weather, and the time had arrived for all the dust and dirt to be banished. The porch, now spick and span, invited anyone who cared to sit a spell to enjoy the nice mild temperatures. As they finished the last of the chores, Verleen heard a car turn off the county road into the driveway.

Turning around and recognizing the car, she paused and waited for it to make its way up to the house. It was the shiny, black car belonging to the preacher of Faith Believers Chapel and it was trailing a cloud of dust behind it...some of which settled on the freshly washed porch floor. Verleen felt a flash of irritation but kept her face impassive as she stood watching the vehicle approach. *What in tarnation? Why is that man coming around here pestering me?*

Before the car came to a complete stop, Grady Turner shot out of the passenger seat and came around the front of the vehicle. To say he appeared to be incensed would be an understatement. He was minutes away from self combustion. "Where is she?" he demanded placing his hands on his hips.

Verleen set down the cleaning supplies and shooed Calvin inside the house. She said quietly but firmly, "Calvin, go in your room and shut the door. Don't come out until I tell you to. Understand me?"

Calvin nodded, slipped through the screen door and into his room, but left the bedroom door partly open so he could hear everything that happened at the front of the house.

The preacher got out of the driver's seat exhibiting a much calmer manner and removed his hat. "Now, Grady, get a-hold of yourself. There's no reason to go flying off the handle."

Grady ignored the preacher's advice and addressed Verleen once again. "I asked you a question. Where. Is. She?" He enunciated each word as if she were hard of hearing or just plain simpleminded.

Verleen stood looking down at the men from her place on the porch. She crossed her arms and took several seconds to answer. "Grady Turner, who did you lose this time?" Her voice was quiet and casual as if she were discussing the weather.

Grady started forward as though to climb the steps but the preacher caught his arm, restrained him, and muttered reassurances in his ear in an obvious attempt to control the situation.

While Grady glared furiously at Verleen, the other man spoke up, "Good morning, Miz Jackson. Grady here is looking for Sally. She and the kids haven't been home in a few days and he's real concerned about their well being." His voice carried a patronizing tone like a snake oil salesman and his demeanor fooled Verleen not one whit.

She just stood expressionless and said nothing in return.

Her silence infuriated Grady and escalated his already bad mood. Unable to contain himself, he blurted out, "I know she's here! This is where she ran to last time I---" he sputtered, suddenly realizing what he had been about to say.

"The last time you broke her arm and bruised her up so bad I had to take her to the hospital?" Verleen asked in a voice that conveyed contempt. "Isn't that what you was about to say?"

"You old woman, you have interfered with me and my wife and kids for the last time!" Grady threatened, his face flushing red.

Taking on the role of mediator, the preacher took a step forward to put himself closer to the porch and between the two. Using a tone of authority, he spoke to Verleen as if to set her straight. "Now, Miz Jackson…I think the good Lord frowns on people who come between a man and his wife. It's just not proper. What God put together let no man put asunder. A woman needs to know her place in this world…the one God gave her. Sally should be home with her loving husband."

Home with a man who loves with his fists?

He seemed to be on a roll. He continued with his voice taking on that "pulpit enthusiasm", a trademark of southern preachers. "The Lord said it's not good for a man to be alone and he made him a helpmate. According to the Good Book, the wife it to submit to her husband. Now this family is being torn apart with others getting involved who have no place in their business. I suggest you send Sally and the kids home where they belong. It's evident that Grady is suffering greatly without his family."

I do believe he plans on passing the collection plate now that he has delivered a sermon…but he ain't gonna like what I have as an offering.

Grady, growing increasingly impatient, began kicking the ground with the toe of his boot and pacing back and forth in front of the car.

Verleen put a thoughtful expression on her face as if considering the preacher's words, but when she spoke her voice was coldly direct and carried a tone of disgust. "I can promise you the good Lord doesn't want Sally and her half-starved kids to live with this raging drunk. I think you'd best take this hung-over idiot with you and go study your Bible some more, preacher man. I can smell the liquor coming off both of you."

Because both men easily manipulated people, one using words and the other his fists, her reply was like ice water thrown into their faces. Devlin Connors' expression was first one of disbelief and then quickly turned to anger as he realized the old woman was not the least bit intimidated by either of them.

Verleen had had enough of these two uninvited, sorry excuses for men so she just threw more gas on the fire. "I'm just wondering if the members of your church would think it **proper** if they knew you spent your Saturday nights hanging out with the likes of Grady Turner here, drinkin' and gamblin' in the back room of Boudreaux's Bar in Louisiana instead of at home preparing your Sunday morning sermons."

Devlin Connors started moving toward the steps with Grady close behind. "Now see here, you've got no cause to be talking to me like that---"

After delivering her last statement, Verleen calmly took a step back through the screen door, reached up above the doorframe, and grabbed the shotgun that she kept hanging there. The two enraged men were met at the top of the steps with the business end of the gun leveled chest high.

"Preacher man, I done told you to take this piece of trash and git off my property," Verleen said quietly.

Both men had came to a screeching halt and stood there uncertainly.

She poked Devlin Connors in the chest with the barrel. "You're trespassing. Now git!"

The men hesitated a moment too long so Verleen pulled the hammer back with a click and let out a loud sigh. "Y'all gonna make me dirty up my nice, clean porch."

Her cool tone was unnerving and helped to make up their bewildered minds. They turned tail and ran for the car in a panic, almost shoving each other down in the process, while extremely loud cuss words accompanied their frenzied flight.

Who knew a preacher could have such an improper vocabulary? She kept the gun up to her shoulder and sighted down the barrel as the car quickly reversed in the yard, mowing down her favorite rose bush with its back tires.

"That does it," Verleen grumbled to herself.

As the car started moving down the driveway, she pulled the trigger, firing birdshot over the vehicle causing it to speed up considerably. They hit the county road going so fast they overshot and veered through a ditch on the far side for several yards before they lurched back onto the dirt road, fishtailing the back end for several seconds and then finally gaining control.

Verleen shook her head in annoyance. "Slow learners," she muttered under her breath.

Calvin tiptoed from his place at the living room window back to his room where he was sitting innocently on his bed playing with his toys where Verleen found him minutes later.

"Are you okay, sweetie?"

Calvin just nodded.

"I hope the gunshot didn't startle you. There was some varmints that needed scaring off. Everything is fine. You can come out now."

Calvin followed Verleen into the living room and she pointed to the gun which was back in place over the front door. "My husband, Elmer, gave that shotgun to our boy, Billy. When you live on a farm in the country, a gun is useful for lots of reasons. It's kept high up on the wall because children should never play with guns. When you're older, I'll teach you how to shoot and we'll go squirrel huntin' together just like Elmer and Billy used to do. We'll cook us up a mess of fried squirrel with rice and gravy. That's Mistah John's favorite. At other times, a shotgun comes in handy when a fox or some other wild animals get into the hen house and start killin' our chickens."

Calvin looked up at her in all seriousness when the chickens were mentioned. He gave a short, curt nod at her explanation.

"Why don't you run outside and play for a while and then we'll have lunch out on the porch."

Calvin headed for the back door enthusiastically and Verleen crossed the kitchen to watch him from the window over the sink. As he ran out into the spring sunshine and headed for the tire swing, his voice came drifting faintly on the breeze. "No worries, Nana Vee. Those varmints won't be back."

She stared out the window wondering if she really heard his remark. She chuckled to herself. *Probably my imagination...my ears are still ringing from that shotgun blast.*

Chapter 16

"Calvin, I need two dozen eggs for Mr. Jenkins." Verleen stood in the yard visiting with the old gentleman through the rolled-down window of his truck. Calvin, who had been sitting on the front porch, took off into the house to fetch them.

"How is the missus?" Verleen asked politely.

"She's alright. We just don't get out and about like we used to. I guess we are just slowing down with age," Mr. Jenkins replied. "We sure did enjoy the homemade butter you brought us a while back. The missus used to make it but we lost our supply of fresh milk when we sold the last of our cows a few years ago."

"The boy and I will bring some more by next time we are out your way," she offered.

"The wife and I would be obliged…here comes your boy now."

Verleen turned and took the cartons from Calvin and handed them in through the truck window while Mr. Jenkins handed some coins to Verleen.

"If you need eggs and don't feel like leaving the house, it would be no trouble to run them over to you. I do believe there must be a secret ingredient in the chicken feed lately 'cause my hens are laying eggs like crazy. They have doubled their output lately so we have plenty. Just give me a call when you need more," she said helpfully.

"Yes, ma'am, will do," he said and then backed up his truck and puttered down the driveway.

Handing the coins to Calvin, Verleen said, "Run put this in the bowl on the kitchen table right now. If one of us puts it in our pocket, it will just end up in the washing machine later on."

Calvin grinned up at her and then headed into the house clutching the money. Verleen watched him go taking note of the thinning fabric on his jeans. *Them britches are shore raggedy. We gonna be seeing his backside soon and that pair is too frayed for patching. Guess we better make a trip over to Berryville this week and buy that boy some new clothes.* She sighed audibly. *As bad as I hate to admit it, Gracie is right.*

He is wearing out them clothes...not growing out of them like he should be. If he doesn't start showing some growth soon, I'll have to take him to Dr. Moore over in---"

Her thoughts froze abruptly as she realized she couldn't show up at a medical facility with Calvin in tow. A doctor would ask questions concerning the little feller that she wasn't prepared to answer. Drawing attention to Calvin being in her care was really risky business, and it was best avoided at all cost.

They spent the rest of the day on chores, given that the small farm required continuous work. Calvin fed and watered the chickens having already gathered the eggs right after breakfast as was his habit. The garden needed tending again since the weeds always seemed to grow faster than the vegetables and that took up a large portion of their time.

Verleen stood at the kitchen counter skimming the cream off the top of the milk Bessie produced earlier in the day. Now she could make some fresh butter for her customers. Looking out the kitchen window, she spied Calvin hurriedly crossing the yard and something in his demeanor caught her attention. A few seconds later, he came into the kitchen slamming the screen door. "Heavens to Betsy, child...what's the matter?"

Calvin headed straight toward her with something clutched protectively in his hands; he stretched up his arms and opened his palms to reveal a tiny baby rabbit.

"Oh, you shouldn't have picked it up, Calvin. Let's hurry and go put it back where you found it before its mother returns." Verleen headed out the door with Calvin close behind. "It's not a good idea to pick up the babies of wild animals. Most times, the human smell you leave behind on them confuses the mother and she will abandon the baby thinking it belongs to someone else. Show me where you found it."

Calvin took the lead and headed to the edge of the back yard stopping at a small hole in the tall grass. Verleen looked at the rabbit's nest and then around in the tall grass and her heart sank. There were bits of bloody fur caught in the surrounding grass. "Uh, oh...I think a coyote or fox has already found the mother and any other babies."

Glancing down she saw the sad look on Calvin's face and she sighed heavily. "We'll take it back to the house but it's awfully little. Come on."

In the kitchen once more, Verleen got a shoe box and lined it with an old, clean cup towel and had Calvin gently place the baby rabbit inside. She then punched holes in the lid. "It's used to a quiet, dark place and we have to handle it as little as possible. It's going to need goat's milk once a day. I'm sure I can get some from the Welch's farm down the road."

The small boy was looking solemnly down at the tiny creature in the box. "Don't get too attached to it, Calvin. Most of these babies can't live without their mothers for the first several weeks of their lives. My son, Billy, and I tried to save lots of baby squirrels and birds that fell out of the nests high in the trees. I can't remember very many that lived. If it does live, we'll have to turn it loose in the yard as soon as it's big enough. We can't keep it. It's supposed to live in the wild. Do you understand?"

Calvin's mouth turned down in sadness and his eyes glistened with extra moisture. Verleen hugged him tight. "Dying is a part of living, sweetie…guess that's something you got to start learning now…as hard as that is for someone as young as yourself. Go fetch the heating pad. We need to keep him warm since he doesn't have any other rabbits to snuggle up with in a nest."

Calvin returned with the heating pad, and Verleen plugged it in and placed half of the box on it, turning it on the lowest setting. "Close the lid now and we'll leave the box on the kitchen table where we can peek in on him now and then…but remember what Nana Vee said…no touching except for feeding him."

Calvin nodded wordlessly in agreement and went outside to sit on the steps where Boone came over and flopped down beside him. The next time Verleen glanced out the window, the boy was sailing through the air on the tire swing. Ever-faithful Boone sat by the base of the tree watching.

The next day dawned bright and clear and promised to be gorgeous. The nights were still slightly cool with the days turning very warm by noon. At midmorning Verleen was puttering around the kitchen when she heard a car coming up the drive. *Another egg customer I'll just bet!* Stepping out onto the front porch, she was slightly surprised to see the local constable's cruiser roll gently to a stop.

The man in uniform unfolded his long legs and slowly got out of his car. He didn't speak at first but casually glanced around Verleen's neatly groomed front yard. Strolling up to the bottom step of the porch, he removed his cowboy hat and glanced up at her. "How do, Miz Vee. I thought I'd better stop by for a little visit."

Chapter 17

"Tommy Lee Boyd, it's good to see you." Gesturing to a rocker, she continued, "Come on up and take a load off. I just put the coffee pot on…let me get us a cup. Still take a bit of cream in your coffee?"

"Yes, ma'am, I sure do," he replied with a smile.

Verleen hustled into the house and quickly filled two cups and set out a plate of cookies. Speaking to Calvin who was sitting at the table peeking into the rabbit's shoe box, she said, "In a few minutes, wash your hands and bring out that plate of molasses cookies. We've got company."

Pushing the screen door open with her hip, she handed the constable one of the cups of coffee and settled into the other rocker herself. "I just knew you were an egg customer when I heard your car."

"I saw your sign out by the road. Your business taking off, is it?" the man asked between sips of coffee.

"I want you to know it's booming," Verleen replied happily. "Everything is perking along. Bessie is giving lots of milk…that's some of her fresh cream in your coffee, by the way…the chickens are laying up a storm and the garden is flourishing as we speak."

"Glad to hear it, Miz Vee. You gonna be selling vegetables out on the highway again this year?"

"With summer coming on and the nights starting to warm, I should have a really good crop for those city folks," she confirmed.

"Good, my kiddos loved that corn I got from you last year."

"And how are all your bunch? Wife and kids doing alright?"

"Everyone is fine. My oldest girl is graduating this year and then will be off to college in the fall."

"Oh, I know that makes y'all proud. Can't believe she's almost old enough to leave home."

Calvin chose that moment to come through the door carefully carrying the plate of cookies which he handed to Verleen. She set the plate on the small table between the rockers saying, "Try one of these molasses cookies. They are quite tasty with coffee…Calvin here made them himself. He is right handy in the kitchen."

The lawman took a generous bite of a cookie and followed it with a sip of coffee. "These are delicious…and you say this little feller baked these?"

"He sure did."

They all three nibbled quietly on the cookies for several moments. Sitting on the top porch step, finished with his cookie, Calvin pulled a small toy tractor from his pocket and began playing quietly, seemingly lost in his own world.

Nodding in Calvin's direction, Constable Boyd asked in a soft voice, "Another stray that's ended up at your door, Miz Vee?"

"Yep, the little feller is staying with me for a while."

The man chuckled, "It's not the first one you've taken in over the years. Speaking of which…Grady Turner seems to have the impression that you're hiding his wife and kids from him."

"Sally and her four young'uns?" she asked incredulously. "Where in the world would I put 'em?"

"He showed up at my office a few days ago screaming and carrying on, insisting I come out and search your place."

"Well, have at it, Tommy Lee. I want you to be able to go back and tell that raging imbecile they're not here."

"No need, Miz Vee. It's obvious they are nowhere around here. Do you have any idea where they might have gotten off to?"

Calvin kept playing quietly but Verleen knew he was listening.

Her voice was level and straightforward when she answered. "I honestly don't know where she and those kids are. I just hope she has enough sense to stay gone."

"You and me both, Miz Vee. Grady Turner's dealt his family plenty of misery in the past so I don't blame them if they've cut and run. I hope they are a million miles from here. Grady will just have to find someone else to torment. He wanted to file a complaint on you but I wouldn't let him."

"On me? What for?"

"He claims you fired a gun at him."

"Did he have any bullet holes in him?"

"Not that I could see."

"Well, I obviously didn't shoot **at** him, 'cause I always hit what I'm aiming for," she replied flippantly.

Constable Boyd was obviously enjoying this exchange. "Lord knows that's true. We were all glad you stopped participating in the annual turkey shoot a while back because you won five years in a row. When you dropped out, the rest of us finally had a fighting chance. I guess the real question is…did you fire a gun in his direction?"

"Oh, yeah…I just popped off a warning shot over the car," she replied in a careless tone with a slight shrug.

"As they were leaving?"

"They weren't moving fast enough."

"Grady had that preacher feller with him?"

"Yep," she confirmed in a voice that carried contempt.

"Was that absolutely necessary, Miz Vee?"

With a thoughtful look on her face and a certain innocence in her voice, she explained, "Well…I am a helpless, elderly, widow woman living out here alone and they was trespassing and wouldn't leave 'til I pointed the shotgun at 'em."

At this point, the man struggled to keep a straight face. "Miz Vee, you are in no way helpless or what I would consider elderly---"

"Tell that to my bones when I try to get out of the bed in the morning," she muttered to no one in particular.

"But you are alone…so to speak," he said glancing in Calvin's direction. "Why didn't you just pick up the phone and call my office if you felt threatened?"

"The gun was closer than the phone," she said simply.

Tommy Lee lost control at that point and laughed for several moments. Shaking his head he said, "Miz Vee, you are something else. You won't be having any trouble from Grady Turner any time soon. I locked him up for being drunk and disorderly and plan on keeping him for a week or two. Do you want to come down and file a trespassing charge?"

"Nah…I think he got the message. What about that preacher feller? He get locked up, too?" she asked hopefully.

"He didn't kick up quite the ruckus Grady did and made himself scarce when he saw me slap the handcuffs on his companion. I think we've seen the last of him."

"Good riddance!"

Constable Boyd nodded in agreement. "I guess I'd better be getting along," he said rising from his chair.

"Just a minute, Tommy Lee. Calvin, run in and get a jar of that mayhaw jelly from the pantry for Constable Boyd."

The little boy was back in a flash and handed the jar to the tall man as he headed down the porch steps and toward the cruiser.

"Tell your wife I said hello and try some of that jelly on some hot biscuits. Ain't nothing better for breakfast," she said.

He opened the car door and paused for a moment. "We will sure enjoy this. Thank you much. Oh…and try not to shoot at anyone this week, Miz Vee."

Verleen smiled and waved her goodbye as he closed the car door. "I'll try, sir, but you're sure taking all the fun out of life," she said under her breath. Looking down at Calvin at her side, she gave him a wink and a big grin.

Chapter 18

"I'm sure glad y'all were free to come over for a visit. Henry has not stopped pestering me since he got here a few days ago. He and Calvin hit it off last time they played together and that's all he talks about. It's Calvin this and Calvin that," Gracie remarked.

She and Verleen were sitting in Gracie's living room with a box fan aimed at them and turned on high to stir the air. The days were really warming now creating excellent growing conditions for the vegetable garden, but the climbing temperatures punished most of the country folks living without air conditioning.

Verleen nodded at the television and asked, "What in the world are you watching?"

Gracie's face lit up, "It's a soap opera that's real popular. It's called *All My Children*. I watch it every day. See that young lady with the dark hair? That's Erica Kane. She's a real troublemaker and gets herself into some fine messes. She can't ever leave well enough alone…"

Gracie continued to drone on about the troubles of the inhabitants of Pine Valley as Verleen grew impatient with the topic that interested her not in the least.

She interrupted Gracie's long explanation of the show's storyline. "Can we turn that off?" She pointed at the television. "It's loud enough in here with the fan in the corner."

Gracie promptly turned down the volume but left the television on so she could keep one eye on it. "Yep, fan weather has arrived. I'm afraid we're gonna have another hot summer this year."

"It's Southeast Texas, Gracie. All our summers are hot. It's just a question of how hot it's gonna get," Verleen remarked brusquely.

"Well, I just don't like it when it gets as hot as blue blazers."

"Blue blazes…the term is blue blazes," Verleen pointed out to her friend.

"Naw, I have a blue blazer that is too hot to wear in the summer and that's disappointing 'cause I think it makes me look slim and it goes with so many of my nice dresses."

"Lord, give me patience," Verleen implored while looking up at the ceiling.

Gracie rattled on undaunted by Verleen's remarks. "It is rather warm to be in the house. Let's go sit on the porch with some lemonade and check on the boys in the yard."

They stopped in the kitchen for lemonade and then settled on the back porch. It was slightly cooler with a light breeze drifting across the yard. The porch ceiling fan turned lazily and that helped somewhat. The boys played on the swing set that graced the back yard as did a tree house and a sand box. Various toys sat in the deep shade of the trees attesting to the number of grandchildren with whom Gracie and her husband were blessed.

"Y'all got enough toys for the young'uns?" Verleen asked sarcastically. "Must be quite an undertakin' to mow around all this stuff."

Gracie chuckled, "It does keep the grandkids occupied when they come to visit."

Verleen surprised herself feeling slightly jealous of her friend's good fortune in having lots of offspring.

"Cathy feeling alright these days? That baby should be due pretty soon if I remember correctly," said Verleen referring to one of Gracie's daughters.

"Yep, baby should arrive about middle of August," Gracie confirmed.

"What's this, her fourth?"

"Fifth," Gracie corrected.

"How she and her husband gonna feed all them kids?" Verleen asked.

Gracie shot a sharp look in Verleen's direction. "They'll feed them just fine, Vee. Her husband has a good job in Berryville and they've done alright so far with the kids they've got."

Verleen just raised her eyebrows and continued to sip her lemonade.

"Hey, did you hear about that new preacher?" asked Gracie.

"What new preacher?"

"The one down at the Faith Believers Chapel."

"What about him?"

"He done left town taking the church's building fund with him."

"Imagine that," Verleen remarked flatly.

"Yep, didn't leave so much as a penny behind."

"Can't say I'm surprised," Verleen remarked sourly.

"Some folks around Lolly Springs think he run off with Grady Turner's wife."

Verleen choked on her lemonade. She coughed for several minutes before she could manage any words.

"Why in the world would anyone think Sally would run off with the likes of him?" she asked in disbelief.

"Well…they both disappeared about the same time."

"And you think some greedy, self-centered wolf in sheep's clothing would want to take on a beat-up woman with four kids?"

"Well…I didn't say that I believed that…it's just what some folks are saying…when you put it that way it does sound kind of ridiculous," Gracie said apologetically.

Verleen snickered. "Ain't that just like a small town? They catch a rumor here and there and then can't wait to weave it into a story to pass around as truth."

"What's this I hear about some trouble between you and Grady Turner?"

"Oh…where did you hear that? Your Sunday school class discussing my business again?" she asked sourly.

"No, Grady Turner himself told anyone who would listen that you was keeping Sally and his kids out at your place."

"Well…which is it, Gracie? Am I holding them hostage in my basement dungeon or have they left town with that preacher feller?" she said in a voice that conveyed her grouchy mood.

"Don't get mad at me, Verleen."

"I'm not mad at you. I'm just sick and tired of the stupidity of some people. They sit around trying to make a soap opera of everything that goes on around here."

"I don't do that," Grace replied firmly. "What in the world is wrong with you, Vee? I've never seen you in such a foul temper."

"I'm just tired of these…of these…just tired, Gracie." Her voice had calmed down and lost its sound of irritation. "I'm sorry. I'm just not feeling myself today. I don't think I've been sleeping well. I woke up this morning feeling exhausted before my feet hit the floor."

"Maybe you should make an appointment with the doctor and let him have a look see," Gracie offered.

"Oh, I'll be fine. I think I'm a little worried about Calvin…maybe that's why I'm not sleeping so well."

Obviously having a wonderful time, the boys were whooping and hollering from the tree house.

Gracie glanced in that direction. "I noticed the little feller still hasn't grown an inch or put on any weight. He seems…exactly the same…since he first arrived."

Verleen let out a heavy sigh. "Look at him. Those two little boys were the same size when they met and now Henry's several inches taller than Calvin."

"That is worrisome but he seems to have an appetite. Sooner or later, he should take to growing as long as he's getting plenty of nourishment." With a great amount of tact, she voiced her real concern. "What bothers me is his inability…or refusal…to talk."

Verleen looked at Gracie in confusion. "But he does talk, Gracie…I mean…not a lot. He's not exactly a chatterbox but he's been talking to Henry ever since we got here."

"He has?"

"Just listen."

They halted their conversation and strained their ears for several minutes. The boys were out of sight in the tree house at the edge of the yard but Verleen could hear a muttered conversation between the two boys taking place. Henry would ask a question and Calvin would answer in his quiet way.

"See?" Verleen asked.

As Gracie's face registered confusion, she turned to meet Verleen's gaze. "Vee, I just hear Henry talking up a storm. I don't hear Calvin's voice at all."

Chapter 19

Early the next morning Verleen and Calvin loaded up the truck and headed to Gracie's place. Their plan to go mayhaw gathering was best to get underway before the day heated up.

Gracie and Henry were ready to go when Verleen's truck pulled up and they were soon inside the vehicle with it rolling down the county road to the location of nearest mayhaw trees. These trees grew wild in the local forest that was owned by lumber companies who never seemed to mind the locals' practice of harvesting the berries. Mayhaw trees were not cut for lumber and the fruit would just fall to the ground and rot if left uncollected.

By parking on the side of the road and walking a short distance into the forest, the trees were easily accessible. The group carried the necessary supplies and got to work immediately. Verleen gave the boys a stern warning. "You boys watch where you're steppin'. There could be some water moccasins about. It's rather wet here where the mayhaw trees grow and them snakes like the wet areas. That's why we made you wear your boots this morning. Stay close by, keep the buckets handy, and we'll be done here pretty quick."

She and Gracie wasted no time in spreading the sheets on the ground under the outstretched limbs of the first tree. Reaching up to grab the low hanging limbs, they took turns shaking the branches which dropped the ripe berries onto the waiting cloth below. They stopped at intervals and picked up the sheets, funneling the fruit into the buckets. The little boys helped as much as they could and in the meantime chased butterflies and each other around about, never once watching for the snakes that Verleen had mentioned.

As they worked together, Gracie spoke softly broaching the subject of Calvin's parents or lack thereof. "I've kept my ears open to all the talk in town but I still haven't heard anything about a missing child, Vee. He's been with you for months now."

Verleen replied, "I've seen nothing in the papers and there's no mention of anything on the news."

"I just keep wondering where he came from."

"I've just about decided that somebody passed through this area and left him on the side of the road and he wandered into my back yard."

"What kind of people would do that?" Gracie sounded aggrieved.

"No decent human being…that's for sure. It's probably for the best that he's not in their care anymore."

The little boys had moved back within earshot so the conversation was abruptly dropped, and the ladies quickly moved from tree to tree repeating the process until they had all the buckets full. It took some time to carry everything to the truck. Once they loaded all of their equipment and the literal fruits of their labor, they headed for home. After delivering Gracie and her half of the berries to her house, the remaining three returned to Verleen's farm where Henry and Calvin had plans to play for the rest of the day.

Entering the kitchen, Henry spotted the shoe box on the table. "Is this where Calvin's rabbit sleeps?" he asked.

"It's not really Calvin's rabbit. It's wild and we'll let it go as soon as it's big enough," Verleen clarified. "You can look at it but don't pick it up."

As the two boys peeked in the box, Verleen marveled that the little thing was still alive. She had not expected it to survive for the first several days but it had against all odds. She and Calvin had used an eye dropper to feed it goat's milk mixed with heavy cream. A week later it was eating with no problem and seemed to be healthy.

As she bustled around the kitchen fixing the boys peanut butter and jelly sandwiches for lunch, Henry chattered excitedly about the rabbit.

"Can we feed it?" Henry asked.

"Not now, later," replied Calvin.

Verleen turned toward the table with plates of chips and sandwiches. "When we feed the rabbit this evening you can help us, Henry. Close the lid on that box for now and go wash up for lunch, you two."

Running from the room, the boys did as they were told and returned to sit at the table and gobble their sandwiches. Afterwards, as they headed out to play in the yard, Verleen unloaded the full buckets of mayhaws and gave the berries a preliminary washing outside at the water spigot to separate them from the leaves and sticks that had dropped from the trees and had ended up in the buckets. They received another washing in the kitchen sink and two large pots of mayhaws soon simmered on the stove. She would have to do this several times to process all the buckets of berries, but once the juice was extracted, it could be made into jelly right away or frozen for future jelly making.

As she worked at the sink and the stove, she kept an eye out the window for the boys who were playing in the dirt with Tonka trucks. They always got along so well with never a disagreement or argument between them. *Not exactly normal for kids to spend so much time together and never have a quarrel...but then again Calvin's turning up here in my back yard is far from ordinary.* Verleen reluctantly admitted that fact to herself but refused to let her mind delve any deeper into the peculiarities of the situation.

With the warming of the afternoon and the heating up of the kitchen, Verleen left the cooked berries cooling on the stove and went outside with cold glasses of Kool-Aid for the boys. Coming to the porch when called, the two thirsty boys sat in the shade and gratefully drained their glasses quickly. "How about I hook up the sprinkler so you boys can cool off?" she asked the red-faced, sweaty urchins who were covered in dirt.

The boys grinned in agreement and nodded with enthusiasm.

"Shuck your clothes and you can play in your underwear," she said heading down the steps. Minutes later, she had the sprinkler hooked to the water hose and the happy boys dashed in and out of the spray squealing and laughing. Hearing the phone ringing in the house, she stepped into the kitchen and answered it. The caller was Gracie asking if Henry was ready to be picked up.

"These boys are happier than pigs in the sunshine. I hate to interrupt their fun. Why don't you just let Henry spend the night?"

"Are you sure Henry wants to spend the night?" Gracie asked.

"I'll bet he does. What kid wants to stop playing with his best friend and go home?"

"Are you sure? I'd just hate for him to want to come home right about bedtime and be a bother."

"Well, hang on a minute, I'll check and make sure."

Stretching the receiver's curly cord all the way to the screen door, she yelled into the back yard, "Henry, you want to spend the night here at Nana Vee's?"

"Yes, ma'am!" he yelled back emphatically. "Can I really?"

"Gracie, did you hear that?"

"If it's okay with you, then it's okay with me."

"Hang on a minute, Gracie.

"Hey, Blanche Comeaux, is it okay with you if little Henry spends the night?"

An audible gasp could be heard on the phone line and then a loud, distinct click.

"Busted!" Gracie exclaimed and then she and Verleen began laughing uproariously.

Chapter 20

After supper, the boys took a bubble bath in the claw-foot tub splashing themselves clean and giggling the entire time. Verleen settled the boys into Calvin's bed and continued reading the book, *Risby*, out loud. She and Calvin read a chapter each night and thoroughly enjoyed the adventures of the curious dog. She didn't make it past two pages when she realized the boys were sound asleep, done in from their busy day.

They stumbled to the kitchen later than usual the next morning and took their places at the table still yawning and looking a little bleary-eyed. The pancakes Verleen served up got their attention and they began to eat with eagerness as soon as their plates were set in front of them. Right after breakfast, Calvin grabbed his egg basket and headed to the hen house with Henry right on his heels. They returned with the basket full to the brim and the extras being carried in a pouch created by Henry gathering the front of his T-shirt.

"Goodness gracious! Would you look at that?" Verleen exclaimed as she retrieved the eggs Henry was carefully cradling. "It's a good thing our customers all bring their cartons to be reused. You boys sort them out and package them up. I have the cartons already waiting on the table for y'all."

The boys quickly squared away the eggs and the full containers covered a good portion of the table top. When Verleen returned from milking Bessie, she eyed the overabundance of eggs. "We better run a buy-one-get-one-half-off sale today or we'll have to eat supper standing up at the kitchen counter this evening!"

Since it was Saturday, Henry asked if they could watch cartoons and the little fellers were soon parked on the floor in front of the television. Henry found his favorite shows and was soon giggling at the animated characters' antics but Calvin grew bored quickly and wandered back into the kitchen to check on the rabbit which, to Verleen's surprise, had not only survived but was thriving. While she strained the fresh milk into a clean jar, she heard a vehicle pull up in front of the house.

Looking through the screen door, she said, "I do think that is one of our egg customers. You boys run out and see how many they want." They both headed for the front door and she yelled after them, "Be sure and tell them about our sale!"

They were back in a jiffy with Henry announcing importantly, "It's Mrs. Mable Richardson. She say she can't get out 'cause of grout in her foot but she wants three dozen eggs." Calvin nodded his agreement in earnest and Verleen chuckled at Henry's proclamation of Mable's request. She quickly put the egg cartons in a brown paper sack, and as Calvin carefully carried the sack out the door, Verleen followed the boys out onto the porch and down the steps.

"I'm sorry to hear that you're ailing, Mable," she said to her neighbor. "Anything I can do to help?"

"Oh, it's just a flare up. I just can't get around so well when it acts up. These boys are good help around the farm, aren't they?" asked the lady behind the steering wheel nodding in their direction. The boys beamed up at Verleen upon hearing the compliment and she reached over and ruffled their hair each in turn.

"You bet! They are mighty fine farm hands!"

The ladies chatted for a few more minutes before Mabel decided she had better take her leave. A few more customers came by and the boys enjoyed taking their orders and delivering eggs, milk, and butter to the cars that pulled up. They deposited the money into a bowl on the kitchen table and the earnings mounted quickly. By early afternoon, the customers had stopped coming which worked out just fine because they were just about sold out of everything.

"Boys, run out and hang the "Sold Out" sign. It's been a good day for business but we are closing up shop for now and then I have a surprise," Verleen said. The boys were back in a flash and stood in the kitchen doorway looking at her in anticipation. "Put on your shoes and let's head to Berryville," she said by way of explanation.

While the boys did as they were told, she put in a quick call to Gracie to explain that she would deliver Henry back home later than previously planned. A few minutes later, the trio was puttering down the road in the old Chevy truck with the windows rolled down to let in some air and chase out the heat. Reaching Berryville, Verleen pulled into the parking lot of the city park. "Since you boys worked so hard today taking care of egg customers, I thought you might like to come to the park for a while."

The boys eyed the shady, woodsy park grounds with its extensive playground area and broke into bright smiles. Verleen sat in the shade in her lawn chair, and the youngsters were a blur of movement as they played on the slide, swings, monkey bars, merry-go-round, and other structures designed to delight the hearts of children. It was a well-maintained park teeming with other families enjoying the Saturday afternoon. As a breeze rippled the leaves overhead, Verleen felt her muscles relax and she sat and simply enjoyed the sights and sounds of all the children playing with carefree abandonment. Calvin and Henry quickly made friends with the other children although Calvin glanced back at Verleen a few times with a look of uncertainty. Verleen smiled and waved to communicate her approval of their play activities, and he eventually lost his apprehension and joined in a game of chase that soon turned in to a game of Red Rover and finally Duck, Duck, Goose.

She watched all the kids but kept a close eye on her own two boys. She enjoyed people-watching and quickly surmised which children were from the same family and were connected to particular parents supervising from the benches and lawn chairs. Sometime later, the boys wandered over to where Verleen sat and she asked, "Want to feed the ducks?"

"Can we? Can we, Nana Vee?" Henry bounced with excitement.

"I brought some stale bread for the ducks. Let me get it out of the truck," she answered and quickly retrieved it from the vehicle. Standing at the edge of the picturesque pond, they broke the bread into small pieces, and the ducks, which were accustomed to being fed by the park visitors, came swiftly swimming to that side of the small pond. Three other children drifted over from the playground area, and Nana Vee gave them the last scraps of bread to throw to the ducks. She noticed the smallest child stuffed his bread into his mouth while his older brother looked at her with chagrin.

"Sorry, Señora, he doesn't understand," the oldest boy said with a heavy accent.

Verleen just chuckled. She had noticed earlier that these three children were different from the rest of the kids in the park who were obvious locals. These particular children had dark brown skin and thick, black, straight, coarse hair. Their parents had sat all afternoon in the shade at a picnic table and looked similar to the children. The boy appeared to be about nine or ten years old and his thick accent confirmed Verleen's suspicions that they were of Hispanic descent, which was rather unusual. People around here were usually black or white and brown-skinned people were a rarity.

"What's your name?" Verleen asked the boy.

"I'm Manuel. This is my little sister, Rosa, and my brother, Carlos."

"Nice to meet you, Manuel." Before she could say much else, the kids headed back to the playground having lost interest in the ducks since the bread was gone.

As the hours passed, the other parents began calling their children from the playground and families began drifting to their cars as it was getting close to the dinner hour. Before Verleen could retrieve her boys, she spotted Manuel holding Henry's hand and heading in her direction with Calvin trailing behind.

"Señora, this one hurt his knee and started to cry," Manuel announced.

"Well, he sure did," Verleen answered eyeing Henry's skinned knee where blood was appearing. "I think he'll live. It doesn't look too serious." A few tears pooled in his eyes but were quickly drying with Verleen's attention. Taking a Kleenex from her pocket, she dabbed at his knee.

"Thank you, Manuel. He'll be just fine. I appreciate you looking after him."

The boy smiled briefly. "De nada, I look after my little sister and brother all the time."

"I guess this would be a good time for us head out. How would you boys like to stop by Dairy Queen and get hamburgers for supper?" Verleen happened to glance up at Manuel as she mentioned hamburgers and for one split second a look of longing was on his face. It disappeared so rapidly that she wasn't sure it had been there at all.

"Manuel, where does your family live?" she asked casually.

"Just up the road." He pointed west of Berryville. "My family works on the big farms outside of town."

Verleen nodded and glanced in the direction he pointed. Something nagged at her strongly…something about the boy and his family. She glanced over at Manuel's parents who sat up straighter and were now paying close attention to Verleen.

Chapter 21

Verleen thought back to the other families in the park who had called their children over for snacks or sandwiches at the picnic tables, but Manuel's family had not been one of those. She then remembered how his little brother had hurriedly eaten the bread that had been meant for the ducks. Keeping her voice quiet and casual, she asked, "Manuel, have you kids eaten today?"

The brown-skinned boy wouldn't look at her directly but looked down at his feet instead.

"It's okay, honey. You can tell me."

Still looking at the ground, the boy shook his head in answer. "Papá doesn't get paid until mañana…tomorrow," he replied softly in a voice barely above a whisper. "He said if we play at the park all day, we will be too busy to feel the hunger pains in our stomachs."

Verleen glanced back at the parents and put a smile on her face and gave them a friendly wave to allay their fears and they visibly relaxed. *Did they eat yesterday…or the day before? When did they last have a meal?*

Calvin and Henry were quiet, apparently listening to the exchange taking place. "The boys and I have errands to run, Manuel, but we will be back in a few minutes. Do you think you can keep your parents from leaving until I get back?"

"Are you going to call the police?" Manuel asked sadly.

"Why in the world would I do that?"

"Some people are not very friendly when they see us in town," he answered, "so we do not leave the farm very often."

"Manuel, this is a free public park. You have every right to be here just like anyone else. You remember that. Now just don't leave. Keep playing with your brother and sister on the playground. Okay?"

"Sí, Señora," he said rather reluctantly.

"Come on, boys." Verleen hustled the boys to the truck and they pulled out of the parking lot. "Okay, fellers…how about we use the egg and milk money that we made today and have a picnic in the park with

Manuel and his family? Is that alright with you guys? I know y'all earned that money working hard so y'all get a say in how it's spent."

She heard the boys talking back and forth in low voices while she kept her eyes on the road and then Henry piped up, "Calvin and me think that's a good idea!"

"Alright, a picnic in the park it is!" she exclaimed.

"Yippee!" the boys shouted, caught up in her enthusiasm.

"Calvin say those people real hungry," Henry offered.

"Yes, I'm afraid they are."

"How come they don't have them any food?"

"I don't know, Henry, but when God sends you someone in need, you don't pretend not to see."

Their "errands" were rapidly accomplished and Verleen headed back to the city park. She breathed a sigh of relief when she saw that Manuel's family remained there. In fact, they were the only people left in the now-deserted park.

Manuel's face lit up when he spotted their truck and he headed towards the parking lot to meet them. "Here, sweetie, help us tote these bags." Verleen had all three of the boys grab a paper bag and she headed toward the picnic table where the parents sat. The man stood up with a concerned look on his face as she approached, and Rosa and Carlos abandoned the monkey bars and drifted toward them in curiosity.

"Our young'uns enjoyed such a good time playing together that I wanted to meet you folks," she said in a friendly tone.

The man and woman looked at each other in confusion and then back at her.

"They no speak English, Señora," Manuel said.

"Well, please...tell them that everyone calls me Nana Vee and my boys want to have a picnic in the park with their new friends."

The boy hesitated for a few seconds. "Go on," she prodded as she started pulling hamburgers, fries, and cokes out of the bags and placing them in front of the children who quickly seated themselves around the table and were licking their lips in anticipation.

After Manuel translated the message, the father spoke in Spanish and the boy translated for Verleen. "My papá said that we don't know you and that this is not..." Manuel seemed to be searching for the right word. "...necessary."

"Tell him my boys will be upset if they can't have supper with their new friends," she replied waving at the parents to take a seat in front of the food she had placed on the table.

"Sit, sit, eat!" she said smiling and plopping herself down at the table. Unwrapping her burger, she said, "Tell them that it's getting cold." She smiled at them expectantly and began to eat so that they would be encouraged to join in.

After some rapid fire Spanish went back and forth, the parents slowly and cautiously resumed their places at the table. Reluctant at first to touch their food, their hunger won out and they were soon devouring the savory burgers that were a local favorite. When the little ones had eaten their fill, the father spoke to them firmly in Spanish.

"Gracias, Nana Vee," they said politely and ran off with Henry to the playground, inherently drawn to the monkey bars once again, leaving the adults, Manuel, and Calvin still sitting at the table.

Verleen dug through one of the paper sacks and in evident surprise found two more burgers. "Oh, my, I think they gave us more than I ordered."

Calvin gave her a sharp look from across the table and she slipped him a sly wink and placed the extra burgers in front of the mother and father. They started to object in Spanish and to push the burgers back across the table but Verleen cut off their protests. "Manuel, tell them I'll just have to throw them away. I've eaten all I can."

After a conversation between Manuel and his father, the man ate the extra burger and the mother and Manuel shared the second one. When every last scrap of food had been consumed, they all sat back stuffed as the sun began dropping behind the line of trees at the edge of the park.

The father and mother spoke to Manuel who relayed the message to Verleen. "Mi papá and mi mamá say they enjoy picnic in park and wish to say gracias for your generosity."

The man and woman nodded vigorously saying, "Gracias, muchas gracias!" Then more Spanish went back and forth for several moments

"They want me to tell you their names are Diego and Maria Ramos and if ever they can do anything for you, you must just ask. We will be working at Adams Farms all summer."

"And what do you and Rosa and Carlos do while your parents are working?"

Manuel looked confused for a moment. "Do? Oh, Señora...we all work in the fields...even my little brother and sister. They can pick many vegetables since they are short and so close to the ground," Manuel said with a chuckle.

Verleen took a moment to digest that information. It wasn't hard to imagine what it would be like to work long, summer days in large, plowed fields under the hot, Texas sun.

"Tell your parents that I am happy we are new friends and if you ever get over to Lolly Springs, just ask anyone where Nana Vee lives and they'll point the way. Everyone knows me and I'm not hard to find. Y'all come by my place and I'll cook us up a big feast..." This time it was Verleen who searched for the right words, "...a fiesta!"

The message was translated and happy exclamations were voiced around the table by everyone and the adults shook hands.

Gathering the trash from the table and disposing of it in the nearest garbage can, the party began to break up. The little ones came running from the playground and the entire group headed to the parking lot which was empty except for their two vehicles.

Manuel walked with the boys to Verleen's truck and helped them climb inside. "Gracias, Nana Vee. I did not tell mi papá that you knew we were hungry. It would hurt his pride very much. He is a good man and he works very hard to take care of us but this was one of the few times the food ran out before the pay came."

"I can tell he is a very good man, Manuel, because the fine, young man you are is proof of that. If your family ever has any trouble or runs out of food again, call my number and I'll come find y'all." She discreetly handed him a piece of paper and he hurriedly slipped it into his pocket.

In response to her last remarks, the boy fell silent for several seconds and looked away toward the fading skyline. When he looked back at her, he wore a soft smile, "I think that you are an angel God sent to us today."

Nana Vee cackled at that, "Oh, honey, I am a long way from being an angel."

"Well...you are our angel...goodbye, Señora."

"I'm really glad I met you, Manuel."

Closing the truck door and backing up, her headlights flashed across the old, dilapidated car belonging to the Ramos family who were all vigorously waving goodbye with big, friendly smiles and shouts of "Adiós, Nana Vee!" Manuel stood apart on the pavement and lifted his hand briefly. When Verleen looked in the rear view mirror, he was still standing in the same place watching their departure and she wondered briefly if their paths would ever cross again.

Out on the road in the closing darkness, the rhythmic swaying of the truck and the sounds of the tires on the highway soon had the little boys yawning drowsily in the dimly lit vehicle. *They'll probably sleep most of the ride back to Lolly Springs. Maybe Gracie won't be too unhappy that I'm bringing little Henry home so late.* She thought back over the day's events. *It's been a good day. Our pockets may be lighter but our hearts are fuller…and that's as it should be.*

The truck was uncharacteristically quiet and she fell deep within her own thoughts and contemplations about the Ramos family as she continued to drive the shadowy country back roads. They were almost to Lolly Springs when she was startled out of her reverie by Calvin's unmistakable but quiet voice reaching across the darkness. "When God sends you someone in need, you don't pretend not to see."

Chapter 22

The next morning Calvin and Verleen woke to rain outside the windows. Because of the cloud coverage, the inside of the house stayed darker longer than usual causing them both to sleep later than normal. Raindrops on the roof made for good sleeping so when Calvin shuffled into Verleen's room still looking heavy-eyed and droopy, she patted the spot next to her and he crawled up onto her old iron frame bed and snuggled down gratefully, immediately drifting back into deep slumber. Neither in a hurry to face the day at that time, they dozed for another hour in the dimness of the bedroom. Bessie would have sought the shelter of the milking shed attached to the barn by now and could wait a bit, and the chickens would still be roosting on their nests until the sky lightened up some more. It was one of those rare mornings where time seemed to stand still and the little farmhouse was a cozy, isolated world all its own.

Verleen decided to take advantage of the situation and they came to the breakfast table in their night clothes for once and ate cold bowls of cereal that required no cooking or preparation. Looking across the table, Verleen announced, "It looks like it's going to rain all day. Just stay in your pajamas. I'll go milk Bessie and gather the eggs. No use both of us getting all wet."

Calvin nodded his agreement and continued to crunch on his Alpha-Bits. *Probably not the most nutritious breakfast but what's a bowl now and then gonna hurt? Can't wait for him to discover that prize in the bottom of the box. That's a fun part of being a kid...finding a cheap prize in your cereal and feeling like you discovered a treasure.* Verleen quickly dressed and slipped on a rain slicker and rubber boots.

"I'll be back directly, honey," she said before opening the screen door. Looking back she saw him start in on his second bowl of cereal. "That boy should be as wide as he is tall," Verleen chuckled to herself as she moved toward the barn.

The slow, steady rain continued all day, and Verleen decided the inclement weather was a great excuse to settle in and be useless. They watched television until it became too boring and then they listened to the radio, read books, and snacked when hungry, forgoing the usual hot meals that Verleen cooked most days. Old John did not turn up and Verleen really didn't expect him to be out and about in the wet weather.

Stretched out on the couch together, Verleen looked down at Calvin and paused in the book she had been reading out loud to him. "I think God knew we needed a day just like this, little man, a day to slow down and take it easy. A body needs to take a break now and then from all the work…and this good, soaking rain is just what we and the garden needed."

Calvin yawned and closed his eyes and soon was breathing deeply. Verleen dropped the book and closed her eyes, too, while the gentle rain continued its pleasant patter against the glass pane of the windows.

Sometime later, Verleen became aware that Calvin was no longer on the couch with her and she groggily opened her eyes and looked about. He was lying on his stomach on the living room floor turning the pages of an old encyclopedia. He had several other volumes stacked beside him.

What in the world could be in those that could hold his interest? There aren't many pictures in those old books.

While she watched, he ran his finger down the columns on the pages as if scanning the words, not really pausing long enough to look at the few photos or drawings that accompanied the text. She closed her eyes and thought about Calvin's past fascination with the newspaper and now his interest in these books. The undeniable truth hit Verleen like a lightning bolt. *Calvin can read!*

It wasn't completely unheard of for a child that young to teach himself to read. Verleen had seen a news story just the other day on *60 Minutes* about a child prodigy that had not only taught himself to read at the age of four, but was also doing advanced math. *Well, I guess I shouldn't be surprised. Calvin is definitely unusual in lots of ways. It's probably better if I keep this bit of knowledge to myself. We don't need any extra scrutiny from all the busybodies around here.*

Yawning loudly, she sat up and smoothed her frazzled gray bun back into place. "Hey, Calvin, let's go make us some popcorn. I have a hankering for something salty and I think there might be a couple of bottles of Nehi sodas in the back of the fridge."

The little boy looked up from his book on the floor and flashed a smile that communicated his enthusiasm for the suggested snack, gathered up the books strewn about, and replaced them on the shelf in the corner of the living room.

Never seen a little kid so neat and organized...one more thing to add to his growing list of unusual quirks...

Reaching the kitchen, Calvin went straight to the table to peek in on the rabbit as was his habit. "You know, Calvin. I think that rabbit is big enough to leave the box. Let's see what he does if we let him out."

Following Verleen's instructions, the boy gently lowered the box to the kitchen floor and took the lid off. He sat on the floor next to the box and Verleen sat in a chair and they waited expectantly. The little brown rabbit crouched very still at first, blinking at the bright light and then it slowly began to move a bit. Its quivering nose sniffed the air and it lifted its head up to look over the rim of the box. "It's got to get used to the new surroundings before it will leave the safety of the box. I'll start popping the corn," Verleen said.

Standing at the stove and heating the oil in the pot, she could hear Calvin murmuring encouragement to the rabbit and when the popcorn was ready, she turned to find the baby rabbit hopping about the kitchen. She handed a bowl of popcorn to Calvin who still sat crossed-legged in the middle of the floor and she took her bowl to the table. The rabbit promptly hopped back over to Calvin and stuck its nose in the bowl. It would hop a few feet away and then come right back to the boy.

"It's testing the water...checking out its new-found freedom but coming back to safety every few minutes," she explained.

They spent some time watching the rabbit explore the kitchen until it came back to Calvin one last time, curling up in his lap and going to sleep. Delighted, to say the least, he gently put the furry creature back into the box.

"He'll be ready to let loose in the back yard in a few days so we better start feeding him grass and clover from now on."

As the day wore on, the rain slowed to a drizzle from time to time but the sun never had a chance to show its face through the clouds and night came early. As dusk fell quickly, Verleen peered out the kitchen window up at the sky absent of stars. "This rain is not only watering the garden but its keeping the heat at bay and ensuring us against forest fires. If the weather becomes very dry for too long, these woods can become a tinderbox and a small spark would burn everything around here. That's normally not a worry since Southeast Texas tends to get plenty of rainfall, but we have had an odd dry year or two in the past," Verleen mused out loud. Turning from the window, she looked at Calvin who had eaten the last of the popcorn out of Verleen's bowl and was licking the salt and butter off his fingers.

"Let's get our baths and head for bed. All this napping has made me tired," she said.

And that is just what they did. When the rain finally stopped, all was quiet and still on the farm and in the surrounding woods. Boone snored from his place on the back porch as a warm, soft breeze drifted across the yard and rain frogs croaked for more downpour, but neither of the occupants of the little farmhouse noticed because they were nestled in their beds in deep, peaceful dreams.

Chapter 23

The ceiling fan did its best to dispel the heat that was hanging about the back porch as there was no doubt that the hot weather was here to stay. Verleen and Gracie each held a bowl in their lap and shelled peas into the containers, throwing the empty husks into brown paper bags at their feet. Calvin, Verleen, and Old John had picked the peas early that morning as soon as it was light since that was the coolest time of day. They had a hearty breakfast of buttermilk biscuits, sausage, and eggs before going about the rest of the farm chores. Gracie arrived soon after the breakfast dishes had been cleared away, and she and Verleen settled on the porch while Old John headed to the barn. Henry and Calvin raced about the back yard for a time and finally sought the shade of the big sycamore tree and settled down to play on the tire swing.

"While I'm thinking about it, Vee, mark July 4th on your calendar and plan on celebrating it with us," said Gracie.

"Well, alright…I can't wait. Been a while since I've been to a party."

"Try to get Old John to come. He needs to socialize and be around some people now and then."

"I'll try, Gracie, but you know how he is. He's comfortable around you and Henry, but I can't even get him to ride into town and sit in the truck when I run errands. Calvin and I will come, for sure. Is it going to be on Cow Creek again this year with all the family?" Verleen asked.

"Yep, all the kids and grandkids…a cookout on the sandbar and playing in the creek."

"Calvin will really enjoy that and I can't wait to see your kiddos and catch up. Thanks for the invite. What should I bring?"

"Your fabulous lemon cake, of course…and…how about a pecan pie?"

"You got it!"

They shelled peas for several moments in companionable silence.

"What's Old John working on in the barn?" Gracie asked.

"He's trying to get my worn-out push mower started. It mowed fine last week but wouldn't crank yesterday. Hope it's nothing too serious. I just don't have the money to buy another one until my social security check comes in next month," Verleen answered.

"Well, you know you can borrow mine if you need, too. You just say the word and Earl can bring it over."

"Thanks, Gracie. I might have to if that old mower is beyond repair," Verleen replied gratefully. "How is Earl, by the way?"

"He's home for a day or two and is as grouchy as a bear. I think he's just dead tired and road weary. You know they expanded his district and now he's gone so much, I'm afraid I'm gonna forget what he looks like. The company shouldn't put so much extra work on a man who is retirement age. They should have the younger salesmen doing the traveling. Be thankful you don't have a husband that's in sales, Vee. I feel like a widow most of the time," Gracie groused.

Verleen continued to shell peas with no comment, content to let her friend vent her frustration as she so obviously needed.

Glancing over at Vee, Gracie took in her passive expression and then groaned in exasperation. "There I go again…open mouth and insert foot. I'm so sorry, Vee. I didn't think about what I was saying. I didn't mean---"

"Oh, for heaven's sake, Gracie. We've been friends forever. You can say what you like when we're together," Verleen said affably. "I know you miss Earl when he's on the road but he is going to retire before long, isn't he?"

"That's the plan. Won't be too soon for me," Gracie answered grumpily and in the next breath she yelled, "LITTLE HENRY, YOU PUT THAT STICK DOWN BEFORE YOU PUT SOMEBODY'S EYE OUT!!!" She stopped shelling peas and picked up a cardboard hand fan advertising Stringer Funeral Home and began to wave it furiously at her pink face. "I just hate the heat! Us plump gals start sweating first of May and don't stop 'til November…I swear it's hotter than the devil's armpit today!"

"Gracie, what's got you so cross? You and Earl have a fight?" Verleen asked.

"Ooooh, it's just…I'm just…I can't believe---" she broke off abruptly.

Verleen waited patiently for her friend to gather her words.

Gracie took a deep breath and cast a sideways glance at Verleen before speaking. "The other day I was in Berryville at the Thrif-Tee

Market buying groceries and I overheard something that just ticked me off!"

"Well, it must have been something. I've never seen you in such a huff. What in the world happened?"

"I could hear some ladies talking on the next aisle of the grocery store and I heard my name mentioned. It was the Widow Comeaux and three ladies from the Berryville Women's Society. She was telling them that my Earl traveled all the time as a salesman and that he had lady friends in other towns!"

"She just came right out and said that?"

"Well, no…but she implied it." Adopting a snooty tone in imitation of the old busybody, she continued, "She said, 'Everybody knows how traveling salesmen get around so Gracie Sheppard probably has no idea what Earl is up to when he's out on the road'."

Verleen's mouth became a hard, thin line as she heard the embarrassment in her friend's voice and saw the tinge of red climb into her already heat-flushed cheeks.

"Then she started talking about my kids, hinting around that she didn't see how they all belonged to Earl since he was never home for long. It was all I could do not to march over there and call her a liar to her face. I just got my groceries and left. I knew if I confronted her in the store, it would have just given her and those ladies more to gossip about," she explained.

"Gracie, you showed more restraint than I would have…but you're right. Making a scene in public would have made it worse. She would have played the innocent victim to the hilt and you would have given everyone witnessing the scene something to talk about all over town. You did the right thing. The Widow Comeaux never got over the fact that all those years ago in high school Earl chose you instead of her."

"And I beat her out for homecoming queen, too," Gracie said smugly.

"And there's that," Verleen agreed. "She can't stand the fact that you and Earl have a big, loving family while she sits home alone. She creates scandal so she can get someone to pay attention to her. If she weren't so cantankerous, maybe her own son would come see her once in a while. I think he moved to the other side of Texas to get away from her."

Gracie nodded in agreement. "She's just a spiteful, old woman and one day those lies are going to catch up with her…all her turkeys will come home to roost."

"Chickens," Verleen corrected.

"What?" Gracie asked in obvious confusion.

"Nevermind…Since she loooooves to talk and the truth doesn't matter, then let's give her something to talk about. Now listen close 'cause this is what we're gonna do…"

The two friends put their heads together and talked earnestly for the next hour, planning and scheming.

Eventually, they heard the lawn mower motor start up, and Old John pushed it from the barn smiling and waved as he headed for the front yard.

"Bless his heart…he breathed life into that old piece of junk. Maybe I won't have to replace it just yet. What would I do without Old John? He keeps this farm running with a few old tools and not much of nothing else," Verleen sighed in relief.

"And you keep him from starving to death," Gracie replied.

Verleen nodded thoughtfully. "It's a friendship that benefits both of us and besides, it's nice to have another person sittin' at my table come mealtime. Calvin and Old John give me a reason to get up in the morning."

Gracie glanced over at the little boys who took turns pulling each other around the yard in an ancient, dented, rusted red wagon that Old John showed up with one day. "Still no idea where Calvin came from?"

"Nope, but I don't think he's from around here. He didn't recognize any of the Berryville area and didn't know what a piggy bank was. He acts like he's never had ice cream, gumbo, or molasses cookies. I'm beginning to think someone brought him from some foreign country and then abandoned him…either that or he's been living in some secluded backwoods commune until now," Verleen mused.

"Now that would make sense. I wonder if any hippies came through this area a while back and were too doped up to realize they lost their kid. Was he wearin' tie dye or did he smell like marijuana cigarettes when you found him?"

Verleen stopped shelling peas and rolled her eyes at the other woman, "No, Gracie, he had on a dirty, raggedy pair of jeans and a T-shirt and smelled like he needed a bath."

"Well, there you go…hippies for sure," she said with conviction.

Verleen closed her eyes briefly and prayed for patience. "And how would I know what marijuana cigarettes smell like anyway?" she asked rather indignantly.

"You tend to take in strays pretty regularly, Vee. I just thought you'd run into that sort of thing before."

She shook her head in disbelief. "Sure, Gracie, I've got a bunch of beatniks hid out in the barn and as soon as you leave, we're going to break out some bongo drums, recite poetry, and pass around the weed," she said with heavy sarcasm.

"I don't know what you do when I'm not here," Gracie said defensively.

The ridiculous, teasing banter continued this way for some time until Old John, having finished mowing the front lawn, joined them on the porch. The boys drifted over to the porch and Henry announced that they were mighty thirsty, so Verleen hustled to the kitchen and returned promptly with cold drinks for everyone.

As they all sat and sipped on the shady porch, Gracie leaned over to Verleen and gestured with her head at Calvin who was now sporting a purple mustache. "They must have had grape Kool-Aid in the hippie commune 'cause he seems to know what that is."

Chapter 24

The next morning after breakfast, Verleen announced that it was time to let the rabbit return to the wild. She had been careful not to give the small critter a name because that would have encouraged Calvin to become more emotionally attached. She instructed the little boy to carry the shoe box out past the edge of the yard and a little ways into the surrounding pine forest where the grass grew tall and tangled. Old John stayed on the porch and kept a hand on Boone's collar in case he decided to try and chase the little rabbit. They wanted it to have a fighting chance to escape into the undergrowth unnoticed by the dog.

Calvin set the box on the ground, removed the lid, and gently tipped it on its side. The rabbit ventured out, blinking in the light. It didn't seem in a hurry to leave but eventually started hopping away and then disappeared into the high weeds. She anticipated some angst and maybe a few tears from Calvin but the boy's expression remained neutral as he retrieved the box from the ground.

"He's going to have a wonderful life exploring the woods and meeting other rabbits like himself," Verleen explained as they headed back to the house. *Who am I kidding? I'm trying to reassure myself more than him. He's handling this better than I am. I can hardly stand to look at the empty box.* While she glanced back a few times, Calvin never did so the rabbit was off on his grand adventure with little hoopla and the day continued as usual.

They spent the evening working in the garden. Many of the vegetables were starting to ripen and needed to be picked and boxed so that Verleen could set up her roadside stand out on the highway the next day. As they pulled corn and picked tomatoes and other vegetables, Old John packed the produce into boxes and baskets and stacked it all on the back porch, eventually transferring it to the back of the truck. They worked quickly but took several breaks on the porch to cool off.

"Miz Vee, I do think you have the biggest crop ever this year," Old John said wiping the perspiration off his face with a handkerchief.

"I'll admit that I did plant more than usual this time. I figured I might need some additional funds with the extra responsibilities," Verleen kept her voice neutral but tilted her head in Calvin's direction. Calvin seemed oblivious to the conversation and was playing fetch with Boone and the old tennis ball.

Old John nodded solemnly. "I'll help you all I can with the extras. Got to take care of our boy there. He's something special. You just let me know what we need to do. I'll help."

Verleen was surprised to find that her eyes misted upon hearing his words. *I guess Calvin is an orphan no longer. He has me and Old John as his family now.* "I know he thinks the world of you, Mistah John. His eyes light up when he sees you at the back door and he tends to fret when you don't come around for several days."

Old John turned away to watch Calvin in the yard and she noticed that his handkerchief moved from wiping his forehead to his eyes. When he spoke his voice was low and soft. "I had a daughter once…her momma died when she was just a baby. She weren't happy with the country life and run off with a feller when she was 17…never seen her again. I pray eva day that she found the happiness she was lookin' fo'…but if she do come back one day, I'll be here a waitin'. She'll always be my baby girl and I'll be here in case she comes home. I ain't going nowheres." Old John avoided Verleen's eyes and stepped off the porch into the yard to join in the game of fetch with the dog and the boy.

This was the most Old John had ever revealed about his private life, and Verleen was touched that he shared that information with her. It was as if they had now formed an alliance to keep Calvin safe and cared for. Feeling less alone in the world, Verleen realized with a start that alone was how she had been feeling for a long time.

As the evening wore on, she watched her family playing in the yard with a warm sense of contentment and reluctantly called a halt to the playtime an hour later when she had supper on the table. Old John took his leave carrying his leftovers in a paper sack after the evening meal, and Calvin followed him out onto the back porch and down to the edge of the yard as was his habit. While Verleen watched from the kitchen window over the sink, Calvin stopped at the beginning of the path through the woods and hugged Old John goodbye and did not turn toward the house until the old man had completely disappeared into the woods.

Just then the phone rang and Verleen hurriedly rinsed and dried her soapy hands and waited until the fifth ring to grab the receiver. "Hello?"

"Hey, Vee, it's Gracie. Did I interrupt your supper?"

"Oh, no, I was just finishing up the dishes."

"Well, don't let me keep you. I can call back later."

"It's no problem. They can soak for a while. What's up?"

"I just called to make sure that you're free for our big July 4th family celebration coming up."

"Well, I did have several other invites and was wondering which one I should attend," Verleen replied smoothly. Gracie fell quiet all of a sudden. Verleen had gone off script and she found it easy to read Gracie's confusion in the silence. "But you know your parties are the best so I'll be happy to forgo the other invitations in favor of yours."

"Oh…good…good…the kids have been asking if you're coming."

"I wouldn't miss it for the world! You know how much I just love being with all your happy bunch; we always have such a good time! Want me to bring my usual lemon cake?"

"Of course! Earl and the kids would be so disappointed if you showed up without it."

That's right, Gracie…lay it on thick. I can just about hear the sound of quiet seething on the line.

"So, what else has been happening, Gracie?"

"Well, I did stumble across something interesting the other day…but I don't want to keep you from your dishes. I can wait and tell you at the party."

"The dishes aren't going anywhere. What is it?"

"I actually shouldn't say anything…it's nothing really."

"Gracie, you know you're gonna pop before I see you at the get together so tell me now."

"Well, alright…but I didn't really want to talk about this on the phone," she remarked in a cryptic tone.

"It's okay, Gracie. We can talk. **You-know-who** isn't home. She'll be over at the quilting club meeting at Maude Henderson's house this evening. I heard they moved their meetings to Friday nights.

"Well…in that case…don't repeat this…it's really nothing…it's just, I been thinking…"

"Yeah? Go on."

"I've been pondering about how Grady Turner always managed to be drunk in the middle of the day in a dry county. Where do you suppose he got his liquor? He never seemed to run out of it and that old truck of his stayed broke down too often to get him over to the state line."

"You know, Gracie. I never thought of that. You've got a point. He had to have been getting it around here somewhere."

"And where did he get money to buy a bottle? The only person around here to hire him was Pete Miller down at the mercantile who let him sweep out the store and unload the delivery trucks once in a while. Vee, you reckon he had a still somewhere in the woods out back of his house?"

"Well, there's a good chance somebody hereabouts has one but it wouldn't have been Grady. That would have required work and brains and he's pretty short on both. I hear that he was unable to pay his fine to get out of jail, and gave the justice of the peace a good cussin' and that just extended his stay in that fine establishment. The rate he's going, it'll be Christmas before he gets out," Verleen replied scornfully.

"Well, somebody around here supplies all the local tipplers with booze. Somebody smart enough to do it right under Constable Boyd's nose."

"You may be on to something there, Gracie. If they're not making the moonshine here in Lolly Springs, they're real sneaky about bringing it in and distributing it on the sly."

"I just don't know who would be that clever…it's not like you can just sell it on Main Street."

"It's got to be someone who don't care 'bout nothin' but that almighty dollar…someone greedy right down to their toes."

"Hey, Vee…you suppose there would be a reward for tipping off the law?"

"There just might be, Gracie. Isn't it a federal offense or something like that?"

"Well, you keep your eyes open and if you think of anyone who might have the means to be running a liquor business, you let me know. In the meantime, don't tell anyone else about this 'cause we wouldn't want to have to share that reward money."

"I'll put my mind to it but just to be safe, let's not talk about it on the phone again."

"Yeah, good idea. Okay, Vee, I got to run. Earl is hollering…he can't find the TV Guide."

"Tell him to look in the bathroom."

"HEY, EARL, VEE SAYS TO LOOK IN THE BATHROOM!" Gracie didn't bother moving the phone from her mouth before blasting out the message and Vee jumped in surprised. Her ears probably weren't the only ones ringing so she didn't complain.

"Earl said to tell you he found it…and thanks…he said next time he loses his mind, he's gonna call you."

"Tell him I drive all of the men around here out of their minds so he'll have to get in line," Verleen said sarcastically.

That elicited a loud snicker from Gracie. "Oh, yeah, you've got the local fellers all buzzing around like bees to syrup," she said drily.

"You mean bees to---" Verleen was saying when she heard the click of Gracie hanging up. "—honey?" She stayed on the line a few seconds longer until she heard a familiar, faint, distant click and then she eased her receiver back onto the hook. She shook her head in amusement and headed back to the kitchen sink feeling satisfied with the phone conversation that had gone as planned.

Just giving the coyotes something to howl about…I suppose I should feel bad…but I don't…nope, not one little bit…

Chapter 25

The morning dawned reasonably cool and clear but the temps would be rising as the sun climbed in the sky. Verleen parked the truck under a shade tree out by the two-lane highway with the tailgate down to display the vegetables to passing vehicles. She had the produce artfully arranged and angled to attract attention. Now she sat and fanned herself while she waited for the customers to stop. Everyone knew that the city folks drove out to the country on Saturday mornings to buy the fresh vegetables being sold by the local farmers.

Verleen had packed a cooler with drinks and sandwiches, and she and Calvin sat on lawn chairs beside the truck. They passed the time with reading material, a gardening magazine for her and John Steinbeck's *Travels with Charley* for Calvin. Once Verleen realized he could read, she turned him loose in the Berryville Library, encouraging him to check out whatever his heart desired. He was hesitant at first but was soon picking books for all reading levels and sliding them onto the counter for check out. Every two weeks they checked out as many books as they were allowed and he was free to read whatever he liked. He was curious about a wide variety of subjects in both fiction and non-fiction, from history, psychology, and biographies to John Steinbeck novels, cold war spy bestsellers, and fairy tales and fables.

As the day wore on, they busied themselves with customers and their supply of vegetables steadily dwindled. To help pass the time, Verleen and Calvin played a made-up game that she called "Will They or Won't They?" When a car came around the bend in the road, they each bet a penny on whether the car would stop or not. It didn't take any conversation; they just looked at each other and indicated their answer with a nod or a shake of the head. Calvin's pile of pennies was growing while Verleen's diminished. About that time, a shiny, red car cruised around the bend. As Verleen watched it approach, a slight queasy feeling began in her stomach and the game was forgotten. As the car rolled by, the man in the passenger seat lifted his hand in a casual greeting.

Verleen did not wave back. *Just keep on moving, fellers…don't stop here.*

She felt herself relax as the car continued on out of sight and she looked down at Calvin who was staring at her intently.

"You felt it, too, huh?"

Calvin nodded solemnly.

"Yeah, something about those people gave me the heebie-jeebies."

Calvin lifted an eyebrow in question.

"Heebie-jeebies…the willies…a really bad feeling. It doesn't matter what it's called. I've just learned it's best to pay attention to it. Every time I've ignored it, I've regretted it. That's the best I can explain it…and that was a car full of heebie-jeebies."

He nodded in agreement, and Verleen let the matter drop; she was well aware that Calvin understood much more than an ordinary little boy would.

More customers stopped and left with sacks of homegrown vegetables and a welcoming breeze put in an appearance to keep the day from turning too hot. A few locals came by and bought potatoes and peas, and many others waved as they passed not stopping since they had vegetables growing in their own back yards.

It was early afternoon when Verleen surveyed what little remained to sell and announced, "I think it's about time to pack up what's left and head home, Calvin. You ready to call it a day?" Before he had a chance to answer, the sound of a car motor drew their attention.

It was the shiny, red car again driving slower than before. Verleen grabbed some of the crates that were on the ground beside the truck and started loading them into the back. Calvin sprang into action also and started gathering their scattered belongings.

If they see us packing up, maybe they'll just keep on driving.

The car continued on by and she felt her stomach unclench but her relief was short lived. The car was almost out of sight when it did a U-turn and started back at a slow crawl. Alarm bells were ringing in her head and she had no time to question why.

Verleen picked up Calvin and headed to the cab of the truck. Opening the door, she deposited him on the front seat. She held his chin in her hand so that he had to look at her directly in the face. "Listen, now. Lock both doors and roll up the windows but leave a crack so that you can get some fresh air. I'm going to get them to leave but if anything happens…you know, anything that just ain't right…you start hitting that truck horn and don't you stop…and don't unlock these doors unless I tell you to. You understand me? **Don't** unlock the doors."

Calvin's eyes were big but he gave her a quick nod and Verleen heard the door lock after she slammed it shut. Putting a neutral expression on her face, she turned to face the two men who were climbing from the car they had just parked in the grass on the side of the road.

"Hate to tell you gentlemen but I'm pretty much out of everything and packing up for the day." She hoped her tone was discouraging.

They stopped a few feet from her tailgate where she kept loading the mostly empty crates and boxes, careful not to turn her back on the strangers. Too late she realized her cigar box where she kept her change for the customers was sitting on the tailgate in full view. She casually threw an empty crate on top of it and then a basket on top of the crate. She had already made up her mind that if they were after her earnings for the day, she wasn't going to fight them for it. Better they grab the cash and go away than…well, she didn't want to think any further than that.

She paused and looked them over. One was tall and thin and the other was short and round. Their clothing appeared to be expensive and they had city slicker written all over them, but something was off…way off. They wore smugly amused expressions that rubbed her the wrong way and raised her hackles.

"Well, that's too bad," Mr. Tall and Thin said with a chuckle. He was trying way too hard to appear casual while his eyes roamed all around not meeting hers.

Mr. Short and Round spoke up, "I was hoping to buy some squash, ma'am."

"Sorry, sold out and my husband will be here anytime now to help me load up."

"Is that right?" the short one asked mockingly, and he and the tall one exchanged a furtive glance.

"I guess we're out of luck on the vegetables, but I kinda wanted to get a close up look at your old truck. A '55 Chevy, isn't it?" asked Mr. Tall and Thin as he rattled some loose change in his pocket and bounced on the balls of his feet. He didn't wait for her to answer but continued, "I'm into old cars myself as you can see by my 1958 Plymouth Fury over there," and he gestured at the shiny, red car proudly.

Another shiny car…another creepy guy…

Verleen didn't answer or acknowledge his statement nor did she look impressed with his fancy car. Then Mr. Short and Round chimed in, "Say, that's a cute kid in your truck. Is that your grandson? Maybe he'd like some candy. I keep some in the car for my kids. He might want to come take a look at our car and maybe play with the radio."

Not in a million years, you two oily, up-to-no-good...

Mr. Tall and Thin slid along the truck using the pretense of looking it over. He had reached the locked cab door which he now tried to open.

Verleen glanced up at Calvin who was on his knees in the seat peering through the back window and they locked eyes. An unspoken understanding passed between them that went unnoticed by the men.

"Like I said...I've closed up shop and I'm expecting my hus---"

"I'd really like to take a gander at the interior of this old truck, too," said Mr. Short and Round as his companion was now trying the locked door on the other side of the cab.

Right then, Calvin laid on the horn and the tall man jumped back in surprise. His face looked like a thundercloud but changed in a blink of an eye as he gave a fake chuckle. "What a cute kid. Can you tell him to unlock the door?"

Verleen had been careful to keep herself positioned so that both men remained in her line of sight at all times. *You don't turn your back on snakes.* The bad vibes they emanated were so strong that she felt anxious and jittery.

The two creeps kept glancing back and forth at each other in silent communication and glancing down the road to make sure they were unobserved. She knew she had a crowbar in the back of the truck she could use as a weapon if needed, but the real dilemma was whether she would be able to reach it in time. She tried to appear calm so that they would be caught off guard if she had to defend herself. *No one expects a little, old lady to put up a fight.*

Stepping up to the tailgate in a casual manner, she placed a box into the truck bed where she knew the crowbar lie and as she wrapped her fingers around the long metal tool that was hidden from their sight, she sized up the two men deciding which one she would swing on first if it came to that.

Chapter 26

Calvin had apparently decided that if one honk was good then 50 more would be even better. He was now laying on the horn at regular intervals with short and long blasts causing the two men to become visibly agitated

"Can you get him to stop that? It's kind of annoying," Mr. Short and Round snapped unhappily.

"Nope, that kid loves that truck horn and he's got the keys in there with him. He won't open the door 'til he gets good and ready. One time he spent three hours in the truck playing with that horn," she said over the ear-splitting symphony that Calvin was performing.

She took a quick glance down the highway and let go of the hidden crowbar, bringing her hand up to wave energetically at an approaching truck. "It's about time! Here's Elmer now to help me load up," she announced happily.

As the truck slowed and started pulling off the road, the two men quickly decided it was time to leave. Without a word, they hurriedly jumped into the shiny, red car, started the engine, and sped away. Verleen shuddered as the car disappeared and she took a deep breath.

Good riddance!

She knocked on the cab window to get Calvin's attention. "It's okay, little man. They left."

He quickly unlocked the door and she opened it to reach in and scoop him up. She hugged him tightly speaking quietly into his ear, "You did good, Calvin…real good. They're gone now."

With his arms wrapped around her neck, he replied, "Don't worry, Nana Vee. I wasn't going to let those bad men hurt us. I would have stopped them."

"Miz Jackson, I'm glad I caught you."

She turned to greet her elderly neighbor who had climbed out of his truck and was slowly coming toward her. "Mr. Jenkins, you will never know how happy I was to see you coming down the road."

He took in the sight of her and Calvin clutching each other and his expression became one of concern. "Is everything alright?" He glanced back in the direction the quickly-departing car had gone. "Those fellows giving you trouble?"

She set Calvin down on the ground. "They was acting mighty suspicious like they was going to rob me but you scared them off when you drove up."

"I'm glad I came along when I did. Are you sure you're okay?"

"We're fine. No harm done."

"Well, glad I could help. I was hoping you had some corn and tomatoes and that you hadn't sold out today."

Verleen set the little boy into the back of the truck. "We sold most of what we had but you can have whatever vegetables I have left. Calvin, start sacking up anything left in the boxes here for Mr. Jenkins."

"Oh, I just need a few ears of corn and a few tomatoes. I don't need much."

"I have more growing in the garden I'm gonna have to pick in a few days so I don't want to take any of this back home. The weather has been perfect this summer, so my garden runneth over," she joked.

She helped the elderly gentleman put two sacks containing a variety of vegetables into his truck.

Mr. Jenkins pulled out his wallet but Verleen stopped him. "You're doing me a favor taking this last little bit. We were packing up to go home. I've got vegetables coming out of my ears."

The old man climbed into his truck and spoke out the window. "We sure appreciate you, Miz Jackson. The missus and I can't get around good enough to put in a garden and we sure will enjoy all of this. You take care of that little boy and y'all stop by for some coffee soon."

Verleen threw the last empty box into the back of the truck and she and Calvin climbed in. She noticed that Mr. Jenkins did not pull back out onto the highway until she did. *That's what neighbors do. They watch out for each other.*

Verleen steered the truck down the road toward Lolly Springs. "I think we've earned ourselves a treat and I know just what will hit the spot."

Calvin grinned up in agreement.

A few miles later, she spied two young boys walking in the high grass that grew on the side of the road. They carried sticks and a burlap bag and couldn't be more than eight and ten years old. Normally, she would have no cause for concern but her run-in with the creepy men had left her shaken. She slowed the truck and brought it to a stop alongside the boys. She looked at their freckled faces and red hair. "Ain't y'all Bobby O'Brien's boys?" she asked out the window.

"Yes, ma'am," the oldest one answered. "I'm Charlie Joe but everybody calls me CJ and this here's my brother, Danny."

"I'm Nana Vee and this is Calvin. Y'all have come out to my place with your folks several times to buy eggs and butter."

"Yes, ma'am, I remember you."

"What are y'all doing out by the road so far from home?"

"We've been picking up coke bottles to cash in and buy us some candy down at that store," he answered pointing down the road.

"Y'all got enough for your candy yet?"

"Yes, ma'am, we found lots today. Show 'em, Danny." The younger brother grinned broadly and struggled to hold up the heavy bag that clinked with glass bottles.

"What say you boys put your bag in the back and I'll give you a ride to the store? It's full and getting mighty heavy anyway."

"Yes, ma'am, that would be great!"

The boys climbed onto the back bumper and it took both of them to load their bag into the truck bed; then they climbed in the cab since the back was filled with boxes and crates. Verleen pulled back onto the highway and a few miles later turned into the parking lot of a small convenience store. The boys unloaded their bag of bottles and headed inside to cash them in with Verleen and Calvin following close behind. While the boys and the owner of the store took on the task of separating and counting the bottles, the owner's wife waited on Verleen and Calvin who purchased orange Dreamsicles and went back outside to sit at a picnic table under a shade tree. They unwrapped the frozen confections and ate them quickly as they began melting in the warm afternoon.

Sitting at the table, Verleen explained how lots of the local kids picked up the coke bottles from the sides of the roads to cash in for spending money. "Most people don't turn in their bottles and just throw them out the car windows. The kids take a stick and swing it through the tall grass to chase away the snakes and to find the bottles. The bottle will make a clinking sound when you hit it. Never reach down into tall grass 'cause you might get snake bit or you could reach into a fire ant bed. You use the stick to roll the bottle out of the grass. The stores will give you four cents for the big bottles and three cents for the little ones. Those O'Brien boys had a pretty full bag so they likely made out alright."

Just then the two boys emerged from the store with grins on their faces carrying small paper sacks. Verleen waved them over to the picnic table and they joined her and Calvin in the shade. "Looks like y'all made some money."

"Yes, ma'am. We each got a bag full of penny candy and still have some money left over. We're saving up to go to the movies over in Berryville. They're showing *Willie Wonka and the Chocolate Factory* at the Pines Theater," volunteered CJ, the older brother.

"Is it okay for your grandson to have some candy?" Danny asked.

"Sure, that's mighty nice of you boys."

The boys each dug into their paper bag and pulled out several pieces of candy for Calvin who smiled at them. He ducked his head shyly and tucked the cellophane-wrapped candy into the pocket of his denim shorts while murmuring, "Thanks".

"Tomorrow we're going to walk the other side of the highway and pick up more bottles," said CJ.

This made Verleen anxious. "Did y'all see a shiny, red car hereabouts today?...like driving up and down the road several times?"

The two boys looked at each other and shrugged. "No, ma'am...course, we wasn't looking at the cars. We was checking the ditches for bottles," Danny answered.

"Keep a lookout for two men in a red car and if you see them, run up the nearest driveway like you live there and hide. If you have to, knock on the door and ask to borrow their phone and tell your parents to come get you."

"Those the bad people y'all saw today?" CJ asked.

"Yes," she answered slowly. "How did you know about that?"

The two boys looked at Calvin. "Calvin told us when you picked us up off the road. He warned us about the two scary men and told us what they looked like."

Chapter 27

Verleen parked her truck on Main Street close to the sub-courthouse. It was a busy morning in Lolly Springs with lots of traffic and she luckily happened upon this parking spot just as someone pulled out of it. The domino players were in their usual spot beneath the shade tree on the corner. They were retired men who could be found there most days of the week unless the weather didn't cooperate. Four men sat at the table to play the well-liked game called 42 and any extra players sat on the whittling bench, spitting tobacco, smoking, and shooting the breeze while waiting their turn at the table.

People passed in and out of the post office, the mercantile, and the barber shop. *Guess everyone is trying to get their business done before the hot part of the day.* Verleen had left Calvin and Old John doing some chores around the farm and had gone to town on her own. She opened the truck door to climb out but stopped when she saw the Widow Comeaux marching determinedly down the sidewalk. Verleen eased the door shut and watched through the windshield as the old busybody went into the sub-courthouse.

She looks like she has serious business that needs tending. Don't want to get in the way of that.

Verleen decided to bide her time and wait until the widow left before she bent the constable's ear with her own concerns and she didn't have to wait long. Shortly, the door to the sub-courthouse flew open and Blanche Comeaux stormed out dragging the constable along by the sleeve. Verleen sat up and craned her neck to see what was happening. She could tell that Blanche was being rather insistent even if she was too far away to actually hear the conversation. Tommy Lee seemed reluctant but allowed himself to be pulled along by the little, old lady.

The commotion Blanche created attracted the attention of the people on the street and they all stopped to watch the commotion. Blanche and the constable crossed the street and disappeared into Pete's Mercantile and several people followed them curiously. Others scratched their heads and walked on but some people slowly drifted toward the mercantile and stood out on the sidewalk. Several minutes passed while Verleen wondered what was taking place inside the store…but truth be told, she had a pretty good idea.

Minutes later, the door to the mercantile flew open and Tommy Lee came out with the widow in tow. This time she was the one appearing reluctant and the constable seemed rather annoyed. Pete Miller was hot on their heels, red-faced, loud, and angry.

Pete always did have a short fuse and it doesn't really take much to set him off. I can't make out what he's saying but I think someone has pushed his buttons.

He gestured wildly and carried on so much, Verleen thought a stroke might be inevitable. The constable tried to calm him down but wasn't having much luck. A small crowd gathered, apparently highly entertained by the whole ordeal. Not much went on in the sleepy little town, and this was the most excitement they'd experienced in a while. Verleen watched the entire show from the front seat of her truck.

Finally, Tommy Lee took the protesting Widow Comeaux by the arm and escorted her to her car, opened the door, and waited for her to get in and leave before he strode back to his office. Thundercloud Pete stormed back into his store, slamming the door in his wake, and the townspeople dispersed slowly, talking to each other about the disturbance that they had just witnessed.

Looks like Constable Boyd might need a minute to himself before I drop in on him. I'll go by the post office first.

Verleen pulled the truck keys from the ignition, dropped them in her purse and climbed out of the cab but didn't bother locking the door. Nobody in the country locked their car doors because no one had anything of value to steal. You had to leave the windows down in summer anyway or the trapped heat was unbearable. She exchanged greetings with others on the sidewalk on her way into the post office.

"Nice to see you, Miz Verleen. What brings you to town?" asked Mr. Duhon, the postmaster.

"Just need a book of stamps," she answered.

While she made her purchase, they exchanged small talk about the summer heat, Mable Richardson's gout, and the fact that the Faith Believers Church was in search of a new preacher…just the usual small town news. Departing the post office, Verleen headed for the sub-courthouse hoping the constable had dealt effectively with the stress of the previous dilemma and would be receptive to what she had to say.

She entered the building and went down the short hall reaching the constable's small office. She stuck her head into his workspace and was relieved to see he was alone. "Morning, Tommy Lee, I hope I'm not disturbing you."

"Miz Vee, it's always good to see you. Come on in," the man replied.

She stepped into his workplace and looked around. As usual, it was as neat and tidy as the man himself.

"Take a seat. Care for a cup of coffee?" he asked.

"I'm fine, but thanks," she answered.

"And what brings you to my office today?"

"I was on my way in when I saw the Widow Comeaux had you cornered so I waited 'til you were free…"

At the mention of the Widow Comeaux, the constable rolled his eyes and let out an exasperated breath.

"Everything okay, Tommy Lee?"

"I swear it must be a full moon 'cause the crazies are out and about."

"You talking about Blanche Comeaux?"

"That woman must be suffering from dementia. She stormed in here demanding that I search Pete's store for moonshine. She said he was secretly selling it to everyone around Lolly Springs and she wouldn't leave until I went over there and looked into his backroom where he receives his deliveries."

"What on earth?" Verleen shook her head in disbelief.

"She also demanded the reward for turning him in, although I told her there was no such reward even if I did find evidence of illegal liquor. You know Pete…he didn't take her accusations very well…he hit the roof…but she was determined to search his back room with or without me."

"Where do you suppose she got such a foolish notion?" Verleen asked casually.

"She wouldn't say…just kept going on and on about how she should get the reward money and asking how much it would be. You picked a heck of a time to come by. I'm sorry…I don't usually have to deal with such foolishness and I was caught off guard. What can I do for you?"

"I hate to bother you now with all this mess with Pete and Blanche but…" she hesitated and shrugged, realizing that her timing wasn't the best in the world.

"What's wrong, Miz Vee? You never just come by for social visits. Everything alright out at your place?"

"Oh, yeah…everything's fine on the farm. I'll come back when things are settled down around here…" and she started to stand up.

"Miz Vee, you just sit yourself down and tell me what's going on," he replied firmly.

"Well, I just wanted to come by and tell you about an upsetting run-in I had with two suspicious men when I was out on the highway selling vegetables."

For the next half hour, Verleen related the details of the scary incident, omitting, of course, the ominous foreboding that she felt when they drove by the first time. She had learned in the past not to share that part of herself. You couldn't explain it to most people anyway and if you tried, they just looked at you sideways after that.

The constable listened intently with no interruption and when she stopped talking, he asked a few questions for clarification.

"I guess this is your day for dealing with excitable, old ladies, Tommy Lee," she said jokingly and then fell silent as she waited for Constable Boyd's reaction.

He had a serious expression on his face when he finally spoke, "Miz Vee, my daddy and your husband, Elmer, were hunting and fishing buddies for years. I've known you all my life and you are **not** an excitable, old lady. This is certainly disturbing. I'm gonna report it to the sheriff's office in Berryville and then spread the word around here."

"I was too shook up to get a license plate number. I guess I had better start toting my pistol when I'm selling vegetables out on the highway."

"Wouldn't be a bad idea to have Old John go with you from now on. Your detailed description of the men and the car will go a long ways to help us keep an eye out."

"They was more interested in getting their hands on my little boy than the money box. Something was bad wrong about those two."

"No doubt."

"I had better get back to the farm. I've been gone long enough. I'm sorry I had to stop by and make your day even more difficult, Tommy Lee, but you stop by my house soon and pick up some fresh tomatoes for the wife."

"That's quite alright. It's my job to handle this type of thing. I'll be on the lookout for that red car and I'm letting everyone in Lolly Springs know to keep a close watch on their children."

"Oh…just tell the Widow Comeaux…the way she squawks and carries on, everybody within a hundred mile radius will know by noon," Verleen tossed over her shoulder as she sailed out the door.

Chapter 28

Verleen rose before dawn the next morning getting her daily chores done. On canning day, it was best to get started before the house heated up. The way the garden was producing, she had plenty to sell, plenty to give away, and plenty to can for herself. She washed and chopped the vegetables and then cooked them a bit before ladling them into the mason jars sitting in a hot water bath. The process took several hours but preserved the food for the winter months when the growing season was long passed.

She hummed while she worked in the kitchen and turned at one point, surprised to see Calvin sitting at the kitchen table blinking sleepily. "Morning, Calvin, I didn't hear you come in. As you can see I'm up to my elbows in ripe vegetables that need to be canned. Why don't you eat cereal this morning? Here's a box of corn flakes, and let me get you a bowl and some milk."

As she turned back to the stove, Calvin dug in to his cereal. "I can help, Nana Vee," he said quietly.

"I thank you for the offer, Calvin, but you'd best not. These hot jars can be tricky and I've seen them explode a time or two. After you've gathered the eggs, I'm gonna need you to bring a fan in here and plug it up for me. The house is already warming up and it's gonna get a lot hotter in here with all this cooking."

They left the 'Sold Out' sign hanging at the end of the driveway so Verleen wouldn't be interrupted by butter and egg customers, and she worked through the morning to get the vegetables processed and preserved.

Canning vegetables was not nearly as much fun as growing them, but it was necessary in order to enjoy them months from now. It made those big pots of soup possible on cold winter days. Verleen reminded herself of that when wiping sweat from her face and neck with a kitchen cup towel.

As the day progressed, Calvin escaped from the heat of the house to the back porch and eventually to the shade of the big sycamore tree where he played with his toy trucks and planes in the dirt while Boone kept him company. Verleen looked out the window to check on him from time to time. She still felt unsettled about the two awful men in the shiny, red car and hadn't wanted Calvin out of her sight since the incident. While waiting for the water to heat under the next batch of jars and lids, Verleen leaned against the sink and glanced out at Calvin for the hundredth time. What she saw caught her attention and she leaned closer to the screen. *What in the world?*

Calvin had a bundle of brown fur in his lap and was petting the brown bundle and also Boone who had his head on the boy's knee. The brown fur bundle shifted and Verleen could see a nose and ears.

Rabbit! How did he find his way back to the yard? And Boone usually loves to chase rabbits but he's ignoring it.

She continued to watch and strained to hear Calvin's soft voice talking to the animals. Just when she thought she couldn't be more surprised, a small blue bird fluttered down from the sycamore tree and landed on Calvin's head. He didn't flinch or act startled at all as the bird used its beak to search through the brown curls. It sat there for several minutes probing and poking with its small beak and then flew back up into the tree carrying several strands of hair that would probably be woven into its nest.

Verleen shook her head in disbelief. *Did I really just see that?*

Taking glasses of cold drinks with her, she slipped out onto the back porch, careful not to let the screen door slam. She eased into a rocker and sipped her sweet tea quietly and just waited and watched. Eventually, Calvin noticed her and she held up his glass of Kool-Aid. Setting Rabbit on the ground, he untangled himself from the animals and headed to the porch.

Climbing the steps, he took his glass from Verleen and sat on the edge of the porch planks with his back to the house, his legs dangling over edge as he drank deeply. Rabbit and Boone followed at a slow pace, eventually climbing the steps and taking a place on each side of the boy.

"I see Rabbit has returned," Verleen said softly. "How do you suppose he found his way back out of the woods?"

Calvin shrugged and continued to gaze across the yard.

"Funny how Boone doesn't pay him no mind. He generally doesn't let a rabbit in the yard and chases every one that he sees."

Calvin continued to drink his Kool-Aid with no comment.

"Just make sure he doesn't graze in the garden. Folks don't want to buy veggies that someone else already took a bite out of," she said humorously.

"Yes, ma'am," Calvin said quietly without looking around and no more was said about Rabbit, who now had a name and took up residence under the back porch, following Calvin around just like Boone always did when the boy was in the yard.

Later when the day's work was complete, Old John, Calvin, and Verleen sat on the back porch anticipating relief from the afternoon heat. They enjoyed an easy supper of cold roast beef and coleslaw on the porch since the house was still hot from all the canning that morning. The porch fan did its best to stir the air but with little result. Old John was leaned back in his chair with his legs stretched out, chin on his chest, and ankles crossed, dozing off and on. Calvin was on the tire swing while Rabbit and Boone curled up together in the corner of the porch dozing also. Verleen watched Calvin play on the swing while she explored explanations of what she had witnessed that morning. She discarded all the crazy notions that came to mind and remained just as perplexed.

The heat finally began to wane and the temperature became more comfortable as the evening wore on. "How about some homemade ice cream this evening?" she asked the boys. "Mistah John, feel like turning that crank?"

"That sounds mighty fine. I'll get the churn," Old John answered and ambled over to the shed where it was kept while Verleen headed into the kitchen.

Putting fresh milk, cream, eggs, sugar, and vanilla into a pot, she cooked the mixture until it started to thicken and then poured it into the metal can that fit down into the wooden churn that Old John had waiting on the porch. Calvin had now abandoned his play and was watching in interest.

Verleen returned from the freezer with a bag of ice and Old John used an ice pick to break it into pieces that would fit into the space between the metal can and the inside of the wooden bucket. He layered rock salt in with the ice until the churn was full, explaining the process to Calvin as he went. Once it was full of ice and salt, he folded a brown paper bag and a piece of burlap and placed on them on top of the wooden bucket.

"You gonna help me churn this ice cream, boy?" he asked Calvin.

Calvin nodded enthusiastically.

"Alright then…your job is to hold this churn in place while I do the cranking."

Picking up Calvin, he plunked him down to sit on top of the churn and started turning the handle. As he worked the crank, the wooden bucket wiggled and rocked and Calvin giggled as if he were on a carnival ride. Sometimes the ice cream churn walked away across the porch floor and Old John would have to drag it back in front of his chair. Once or twice Calvin had to hop off and let him check the ice and more was added along with salt and then the churning would resume.

Finally, the crank became too hard to turn and Old John pronounced it ready to eat. Verleen fetched some bowls and spoons, the churn was disassembled, and the ice cream dished up. Sighs and smacking lips was the only thing heard for several minutes as the trio enjoyed the creamy dessert and the whole yard was cast in shade as the sun dropped behind the tall pine forest at the edge of the farm and the heat finally abated.

The ice cream was so delicious that everyone had seconds and then Verleen put away what was leftover before it could completely melt.

"I'm full as a tick," Old John said rubbing his belly.

Calvin giggled at his remark and rubbed his belly also.

"I've a hankering for some music, Mistah John. You got your harmonica with you?" Verleen asked.

In answer, the old gentleman pulled a harmonica from his front shirt pocket and blew a few notes before he took off on a rousing version of "Old Dan Tucker". Verleen recognized the tune and joined in singing the words in her off-key but cheerful voice.

"Get out of the way, old Dan Tucker.
You're too late to have your supper.
Supper's gone and breakfast's cooking.
Old Dan Tucker just standing there a-looking."

Calvin joined in by jumping up and dancing a jig on the porch floor boards in time with the music. Old John finished the song and clapped his hands at Calvin's dancing efforts and then continued to play one song after another, alternating between fast, stirring ones and slow, bluesy numbers. As the sound of music and laughter drifted across the yard on the warm summer air, stars began winking on in the twilight and the woods were filled with fireflies that flickered with lights of their own.

Chapter 29

The hot, dry dust boiled up behind the old truck as Verleen and Calvin headed down the driveway. "This is a perfect day for hanging out at the creek. You're gonna love all of Gracie's family. They really know how to throw a party," said Verleen looking down at Calvin. The boy made no reply but she could feel his uncertainty at being around so many unfamiliar people. "You just wait. Playin' in the creek beats playin' with the water hose in the back yard any day."

Arriving at Cow Creek, they parked the truck under the shade of big cypress trees on the bluff and before they could pull the cooler, watermelon, and lawn chairs out of the truck bed, Gracie's sons and grandsons showed up to help. They carried all of her gear to the sand bar on the creek where tables, chairs, and coolers rested under several canopies erected to provide shade. Gracie sat in a lawn chair watching her family who, with the exception of Cathy, played in the shallow water. Cathy had less than a month to go before the delivery of the child she carried and reclined on a lounge chair in the shade.

"About time you got here. Couldn't get Old John to join us?" Gracie asked Verleen who plopped in a chair under the canopy beside her.

"Oh, you know him…I tried, but he's just not in to parties…not like me and Calvin here." Verleen ruffled the little boy's hair as he stood by her chair watching the frolicking crowd in the water.

Henry spied Calvin and came running up the sand bar in their direction. "Come on, Calvin! Come play!"

Verleen gave him a gentle push. "Go on, Calvin. I'll be watching from here."

Calvin hesitantly left the safety of Verleen's side and headed toward Henry who grabbed him by the hand and pulled him into the middle of Gracie's family who were sitting and splashing in the creek.

Cow Creek was the perfect place to beat the summer heat. The sand was clean and white and ideal for building sand castles while the water was shallow, clean, and cold. The adults sat in the water playing with the younger kids while the teenagers entertained themselves on the rope swing that someone had hung from a tall tree years ago. The kids climbed up the bank and grabbed the thick rope in both hands and then jumped onto the big knot on the end using it as a seat. When the rope swung out over the deep part of the creek, the kids let go, shrieking with excitement until they plunged into the water.

As Gracie's and Earl's various grown sons and daughters stopped under the canopies to grab cold drinks from the coolers, Verleen exchanged hugs and small talk. Her best friend had three sons and two daughters, all who were married and had produced a multitude of grandchildren ranging in age from young adult to Cathy's one-on-the-way. While Gracie was content to sit in the shade and dispense drinks from the cooler, Earl was right in the midst of all the activities going on. He played with the littles in the shallow water and to the delight of the teenagers, tried out the rope swing and splashed into the creek with an impressive cannonball.

Gracie and Verleen relaxed in the shade, dug their toes in the sand, and laughed at all the antics of the family frolicking in the water. Verleen took a sip of her coke and glanced over at Gracie. "I guess you heard about the Widow Comeaux's visit to Constable Boyd's office last week, huh?"

"Oh, that story got around town pretty fast. Seems she made a spectable of herself and everyone's still laughing, and I think old, greedy Pete hasn't stopped fuming and threatening a lawsuit for slander."

"You mean a spectacle?"

Gracie sighed loudly, "No, a spectable...someone who is gullible and prone to make a scene. You really need to get yourself a dictionary, Vee."

"You'll have to loan me yours 'cause I think mine must be outdated," Vee said sarcastically. "Anywayyyyy...She must be laying low 'til the commotion dies down. No one's seen hide nor hair of her since that day in town."

"And she missed the last meeting of the Berryville Women's Society...so I hear," Gracie remarked with a snicker.

"I think she's learned her lesson about spreading rumors and outright lies," Verleen said with a great deal of satisfaction.

"Here's to lessons learned the hard way!" Gracie said clinking her coke bottle against Verleen's.

Their quiet moment was interrupted by Calvin and Henry's squeals of delight as they chased each other in front of the canopies and down the sand bar ending up in the water once again.

"How goes it with Calvin? Anything new with his situation?" Gracie asked.

"Actually there have been a few things…" and Verleen launched into explaining how she discovered that Calvin could and did prefer to read at an adult level and followed that with a description of what she had seen out her kitchen window of Rabbit, and the blue bird who were all mysteriously drawn to the boy.

"And you're just now telling me this?" Gracie asked rather indignantly.

"Well, I haven't seen you and it's not like we can talk on the phone," Verleen replied.

"Not privately anyway," Gracie answered. "The truth of the matter is, Vee….he's no ordinary child."

"That's becoming more and more apparent to me and why I need to keep him safe and away from public scrutiny. Once people realize how special he is…well, questions will be asked, the authorities will become involved, and his normal life will be over. Since I have no legal right to him, no telling where he will end up…probably with some pinhead scientists or doctors who will want to test his IQ and maybe study his brain. They'll take him away…and I don't think I could stand that. It would kill me, Gracie…"

"That's not gonna happen, Vee. We won't let it. I don't know all the answers…but…but we just won't. Maybe we should try to get him a birth certificate or something, in case you ever need it."

"Well, applying for a birth certificate would draw the attention we're trying to avoid."

"I didn't mean that we should apply for one."

"Well, how in the world? Are you talking about a fake document?"

"You know I got that ex-lawyer cousin in Alabama who is kind of on the shady side? Well, he got disembarked but that's a long story… anyway…the important thing is he owes me a favor and---"

"He could get Calvin a birth certificate?"

Gracie shrugged, "It would be real as far as anyone around here would know."

"Is this something you've done before?"

"Well…no, Vee, but if that would keep anyone from questioning his background and you being his legal guardian, I'll see what I can do."

"You would do that for me, Gracie?"

"You're my best friend, Vee, and we are gonna do whatever it takes to keep Calvin with you where he's safe and looked after. Ain't nobody gonna take him away."

Just then, Earl flopped down in the lawn chair beside Gracie. "These young'uns are wearing me out! Whose idea was it to have all these kids?" he asked with a grin. "And what are you ladies talking about? I swear you two are thick as thieves when you're together."

Gracie replied with a straight face, "We're just planning our future venture into a life of crime, maybe a bank heist...or some moonshinin'...or maybe even some good old-fashioned forgery..."

Coke shot out of Verleen's nose at that point and her coughing attack put an end to the conversation.

Chapter 30

When the shadows of the trees lining the creek had lengthened and cast shade across the water, the barbecue pit was lit and the smell of sizzling burgers and hot dogs filled the air. Everyone dug in and for the first time that day, quiet descended where the family gathered and ate voraciously. Earl retrieved the watermelon from the creek where it had been left to cool and quickly cut and distributed it to everyone present.

Calvin and Henry sat on the sand together devouring their full plates, and now with slices of watermelon in their hands, juice ran down their chins as they spit the seeds at each other. Calvin had quickly lost his shyness in the crowd of Henry's relatives who instantly treated him as one of the family. Other than giggles and squeals, he hadn't said a word all day and didn't need to since Henry did most of the talking for both of them.

Verleen's lemon cake and pecan pie were a hit as usual and were quickly consumed by the hungry bunch. When the group moved back down the shady bank towards the creek, Verleen and Gracie followed to put their lawn chairs at the edge so that their feet could rest in the cold water. They each held a napping toddler twin who was tired from a day of play. Their chairs were situated far enough from the activity in the water so the youngsters would not be awakened by the noise or splashing.

"Can't remember the last time I held a little one. Sure feels nice," Verleen said wistfully.

Gracie laughed. "Anytime your lap feels empty, you just pay Earl Jr. a visit. With these twins, there's always a crying baby to be held or a diaper to be changed, and now that they've learned to crawl, they are into everything. He and Amanda would likely hold you hostage and never let you leave, and once Cathy delivers, they would fight over you like you're the last chicken wing on the dinner table at the family reunion!"

Verleen laughed out loud. "I have to admit that I often envy you, Gracie. Your life is filled with this big, happy family."

"Oh, Vee, you know a big family also comes with big problems…sometimes there are squabbles…and good heavens, they **are** a noisy bunch…and ditch any plan on going to the bathroom by yourself ever again. Seems the moment I close the door, somebody needs in," Gracie said with a laugh.

"I'm guessing they need to consult the TV Guide?"

Gracie laughed for several seconds at that. "Earl thought it was pretty funny how you could locate his magazine from over the phone. He would be really spooked if he only knew…" and she looked at Verleen and raised her eyebrows.

"Speaking of which…something really strange happened the other day while Calvin and I were out on the highway selling garden produce." Verleen took several minutes to relay the events along with the bad feelings she'd experienced when the suspicious-acting men first appeared on the scene. There was no reason to leave out the creepy part since Gracie was very familiar with Verleen's ability to perceive things others didn't.

"Not the first time your sensing has come in real handy," Gracie remarked.

"The evil intentions of those two just rolled off them like waves," Verleen shuddered as she said the words. "Calvin felt it, too, as soon as I did."

"That would explain some things."

"Like what?"

"Well, the way you two communicate without much talking. I've noticed the way you just look at him and he knows what he's supposed to do. It's like y'all have a conversation the rest of us can't hear," Gracie said.

"Well, I didn't have to tell him those men were dangerous. He felt it just like I did. What kind of people ride around looking for children to snatch? I don't even want to think about what happens to the kids they get their hands on." She shuddered visibly.

"It's hard for us to imagine, Vee, but I'm afraid there is more evil in this world than we want to admit," Gracie said and they sat quietly dwelling on that sobering thought.

"If evil does comes anywhere near me and mine again, I'll shoot it," Verleen said flatly.

"I'd expect nothing less," Gracie replied. "You suppose your highly developed sensing ability comes from your Cherokee Indian grandmother?"

"I have no idea…I guess Native Americans could be more connected to the spirit world than others…I mean, you hear stories…but I never met my grandparents so all that part of the family history is lost to me."

The toddler in Verleen's lap woke up and started fussing so she fetched a cookie for the child. "That's what my visit to the constable was about last week. I was letting him know about those strange men. You keep an eye out, too, Gracie. Tell all your family to be more careful when the kids go out to play in the yard."

"I definitely will."

The baby in Verleen's lap, thoroughly enjoying its snack, left smears of gooey cookie crumbs on her blouse but Verleen didn't care. It was just nice to hold the infant who jabbered and laughed with abandonment when she pretended to eat the child's sticky cookie. After the toddler sibling in Gracie's lap awoke, the parents came to retrieve both babies, and Verleen splashed a little creek water on her hands and blouse to clean up. Then the ladies waded along the creek edge to where Henry and Calvin sat in the shallow water.

"Vee, look at the fish," Gracie said very calmly.

The boys were sitting in waist-deep, clear water watching the fish that were gathering around them…actually, around Calvin. Although the two boys sat side-by-side in the water, it was obvious they were drawn to Calvin.

Small minnows hung suspended in the water all around the boy as if he were their leader, and they responded to his faintest hand movements, quickly adjusting their positions in synch. "This is what you were telling me about," said Gracie very softly.

The two boys looked up at the adults and smiled.

"The fish like Calvin. They been following him all day," Henry said gleefully.

"I can see that," said Verleen keeping her voice neutral and low.

"Hey, honey, gather up the kids and find some seats," Earl said approaching. "Fireworks gonna start soon."

At the first sound of Earl's voice, Calvin flicked his wrist and the minnows quickly disappeared into the current. He looked up at Verleen with questioning eyes and she nodded slightly to show her approval.

Don't let anyone see how different you are, kid. Play it safe.

Calvin flicked his eyes in Gracie's direction.

Don't worry about Gracie. She can keep a secret and she's gonna help me keep you safe.

Coaxing the boys out of the creek, Verleen and Gracie helped to gather up all the kids and distributed sparklers to those big enough to participate. Calvin and Henry ran around the sandy bank with the other children drawing light pictures in the air with their sparklers until they fizzled out. Then the kids were wrapped in beach towels and placed on blankets or in the laps of the adults in lawn chairs. When the family had all assembled on the beach, the guys organized the fireworks and the show began as dusk deepened. Bottle rockets and Roman candles exploded in the air and their illuminated bursts reflected in the water below. The light display eventually ended with one big rocket erupting for several minutes sending thousands of fire stars in different directions. The audience clapped and hooted and shouted, "Happy Fourth of July!"

The party broke up quickly at that point, and tired but happy children were carried up the bluff and safely stowed in the waiting cars along with the tables, chairs, and coolers. Everyone hugged goodbye and agreed that this was the best party yet, and the headlights on the vehicles lit the darkness as all the families headed for home.

Verleen and Calvin rode the short distance they traveled in silence and were soon turning off the county road onto their driveway. "That Sheppard clan sure does know how to hold a shindig! I'm all partied out...how about you?"

"Can we celebrate America's independence again tomorrow?" Calvin asked hopefully in a sleepy voice that ended with a yawn and Verleen smiled in the darkness of the truck.

They made quick work of unloading from the truck only what was necessary and left the rest for the next morning; they were soon in their beds sleeping soundly, played out from the day at the creek and all the festivities that went with it.

Chapter 31

When Verleen finally climbed out of bed the next morning, she was surprised to find an empty cereal bowl in the sink. The absence of the egg basket by the back door attested to the fact that Calvin was already going about his daily chores. She glanced at the clock on the wall and realized that she had overslept some…well, more than a little…quite a lot, actually.

You'd think I'd feel rested having gotten some extra sleep but I don't. I hope I'm not coming down with something. She fixed a cup of coffee and sat down at the kitchen table just as Calvin came in the back door.

"I didn't hear you get up this morning. I guess I was more tired than usual. I can hear Bessie bawling to be milked. I'll tend to her as soon as I finish my coffee."

Calvin set the overflowing basket of eggs on the table and began to package them in cardboard cartons, finishing the job just as Verleen drank the last sip of her coffee.

"How about we have an easy day and just tend to the butter and egg customers that come by? Go take down the 'Sold Out' sign at the end of the driveway and that will let people know we're open for business today."

As Calvin passed by her chair heading for the front door, he stopped to whisper in her ear, "You tend to Bessie and then rest, Nana Vee. I'll take care of the customers," then he gave her a kiss on the cheek.

Verleen shook her head and touched her cheek in amazement. *That's sure to lift anyone's spirits.* Feeling slightly better, she slipped on her rubber boots and made quick work of milking the cow and turning her out into the pasture. Carrying the full pail of milk back to the house, the tiredness came over her again. Calvin was waiting for her on the back porch. When she entered the kitchen, she saw that the boy had already set out the clean milk jars and the strainer on the counter.

"Bless your heart, honey. You're really on the ball. I'm gonna have to give you milking lessons just as soon as you grow enough that Bessie won't step on you."

The fresh milk was soon stored in the refrigerator and the kitchen was restored to its neat order as the customers started arriving. Verleen sat in a front porch rocker and let Calvin deliver the eggs and butter to the customers' cars. He made change from the bowl on the kitchen table with no help from Verleen who discovered his ability to count money soon after she realized he could read.

Occasionally, a customer requested a gallon of milk and Verleen would carry the heavy glass jar out to their vehicle then gratefully plopped back down into the rocker. At noon, Calvin stood on a chair to reach the kitchen counter, made peanut butter and jelly sandwiches, and brought them out onto the porch.

"Don't think I've ever had a tastier sandwich. You do have a way with peanut butter and jelly, Calvin. Now that I know you're such a good cook, I guess it's time you got a job. Maybe they need someone to flip burgers at Dairy Queen. Awww, what am I thinkin'? That won't work…you can't see over the steering wheel to drive yourself to Berryville," she joked.

Calvin grinned at her around a mouthful of sandwich.

"I just don't know why I'm so tired today. I'm gonna lie on the couch for a few minutes. You wake me up if any more customers come by." Verleen rose wearily from her chair and shuffled off to the living room. Once stretched out on the couch, she dozed off immediately and didn't hear Calvin as he collected their plates and glasses from the porch and rinsed them in the sink. With the attic fan running and the windows opened a bit, air was pulled through the house making the temperature tolerable. The partly cloudy skies also helped to keep the heat at bay.

For the next several hours, Calvin went in and out the front door quietly filling orders for the drive-up customers who were accustomed to doing business with the silent, little boy. When they asked about Verleen, Calvin just pointed at the house and they all assumed she was busy inside with housekeeping chores. In between customers, Calvin sat on the footstool by the couch and kept a watch on the sleeping Verleen. When the supply of eggs and butter ran low, he hung up the 'Sold Out' sign and returned to the footstool to keep vigil.

When Verleen finally awoke, she sat up and smoothed her frizzled hair, re-pinning her gray bun into place. Calvin sat across the room in an overstuffed armchair with a library book on his lap. Looking out the window and taking note of the afternoon light, she remarked, "I didn't mean to sleep so long but it looks like most of the day is gone." She began to stand up and realized she was rather woozy and sank back down. She leaned her head against the back of the couch and closed her eyes waiting for the room to stop spinning.

Minutes later when she ventured to open her eyes, she found Calvin standing at her knee with a glass of sweet tea. "How did you know that's what I needed?" Verleen asked with a light heartedness that she hoped sounded authentic. Draining the last of her glass, Verleen did feel better. "Thanks, sweetie. What would I do without you?"

With her head now cooperating, she headed to the kitchen and stopped short when she saw the money bowl overflowing on the table and all the eggs gone. "Wow! You are quite the salesman." Glancing into the refrigerator, she noted her stockpile of butter and cream had been greatly reduced also. "Looks like we really hit the jackpot today. Guess you'd better run out and hang out the 'Sold Out'--- I bet you already have, haven't you?"

Calvin smiled and nodded.

"Boy, you are something else!" she exclaimed ruffling his hair.

They sat together at the table and organized and counted the money. When she gave Calvin his earnings, he ran and got his almost-full piggy bank and stuffed in the additional bills and coins.

"Looks like I had better get you another piggy bank...maybe a bigger one this time 'cause between the garden and the milk and eggs, we are doing a booming business." Verleen took her share of the profit and tucked it into the coffee can that she kept in the back of the cupboard and she took Old John's share and put it in an envelope that would be slipped into his next bag of leftovers. The first time he had discovered the money, he had tried to return it in protest but Verleen stood firm on his keeping it. This farm was an enterprise that took all three of them to work it so they all shared in the bounty...whether it was at the table or in their pockets.

Verleen sighed heavily. "I'm just not up to cooking this evening. Let's warm up the leftover beans, rice, and cornbread in the fridge and have us an early supper."

Just as they were dishing up their plates from the pots on the stove, Old John showed up at the back door and joined them around the table.

Grace was said and they all dug in. "I'm afraid leftovers are on the menu this evening, Mistah John. I had a sinking spell and slept all afternoon," she said apologetically.

"Miz Vee, these pinto beans with sausage are mighty good and there be no need to heat up the kitchen," Old John responded.

"I rarely nap during the day. Just don't know why I was so tuckered out."

Old John and Calvin exchanged a worried look. They also noticed how she just picked at her food and didn't seem to have much of an appetite. She proudly told Old John how Calvin handled the afternoon customers all by himself.

"He gonna be runnin' this whole farm fo' we knows it," Old John said.

"Speaking of the farm…I've been thinking…" Verleen began.

"Uh, oh!" said Old John without looking up from his plate, setting Calvin off into fits of giggles.

"Alright, you two…hear me out. In the past, we've grown pumpkins in the fall and sold them out on the highway. I saw in my gardening magazine where city folks like to bring their kids out to the country to pick their own pumpkins from the patch and take pictures. Maybe we should do it differently this year…put some signs up out on the highway to lead them to the house and our pumpkin patch…decorate the front porch for fall and put up a scarecrow in the garden…make it look real appealing, you know? Maybe even sell cookies and lemonade. Those city folks might even want to buy eggs, butter, and jelly while they're here. What do y'all think?"

Calvin and Old John looked at each other and then looked at her and shrugged. Old John stroked his chin for a moment before answering, "Seems to me we'd be foolish not to try, 'cause everything you touch lately been turnin' gold, Miz Vee. I think it be a right good idea. What you say, boy?"

Calvin nodded enthusiastically.

"Good! I was hoping y'all would agree 'cause tomorrow is the day we plant pumpkins," she announced.

After supper, they hastily cleaned the kitchen and took their baths. Verleen and Calvin headed to bed early in anticipation of the pre-dawn hour in which they would be rising to tackle the pumpkin planting. In spite of Verleen's long afternoon nap, she fell asleep quickly but Calvin did not. He read under the covers with a flashlight for some time and when he finally put the book aside, he lay awake for a long time listening to Verleen's soft snores coming from across the hall.

Chapter 32

As July melted into August on the farm, the summer garden played out and the last of the vegetables were sold out of the back of the truck, with some being given to friends and neighbors or put away in the freezer and some preserved in mason jars in the pantry. The pumpkin plants were coming on and had started putting out small vines that would eventually grow to yield blossoms that would become pumpkins. If the numerous small sprouts scattered across the plowed plot of land were any indication, the pumpkin patch appeared likely to produce a bumper crop for the trio's new business venture.

As typical in Southeast Texas, summer fiercely continued through August with very little relief from the heat. By now, folks, especially weary of the uncomfortable temperatures, longed for the first cool snap that would come in the fall. September finally arrived on the heels of August and the heat wave let up. It was still necessary to run the attic fan and a box fan here and there about the house, but the house cooled off earlier at the end of the day and warmed up later in the morning. Verleen and her crew had planted a small fall garden of beets, cabbages, and assorted greens after the summer garden had been plowed under. Rabbit continued to live under the back porch and follow Calvin around in the yard and Verleen planned to erect a temporary fence around the small garden because Rabbit was still a rabbit after all, and greens could be mighty tempting to the little creature.

One afternoon while Verleen and Calvin were at the end of the driveway checking the mailbox, a school bus came rumbling down the county road and she realized with a start that school had begun. She felt safe that his small size kept anyone from questioning his lack of enrollment in the local school for now but that couldn't last forever.

Maybe I can pass him off as handicapped since he never talks around folks. Nobody pays much attention when people keep their disabled kids at home. He only looks about four years old so that does buy us some time. But then again, one day somebody's gonna notice he doesn't grow. Could be that might work in our favor with people thinking he's got some kind of medical condition.

As they strolled slowly back toward the house, Verleen worried the problem over in her mind. She went back and forth on the matter but reached no solution to the problem by the time they climbed the porch steps. What she did have, though, was a terrific idea of another nature and she wondered why she hadn't thought of it before.

Dropping the mail on the table, she said, "Calvin, go out and give the pumpkin patch a good watering, will you? They're looking a little dry. Careful not to drag the hose across the garden and damage the little sprouts while you're at it."

As soon as the screen door slammed behind the boy, Verleen was on the phone. "Gracie, hey, it's me, Verleen…what do you mean Verleen who? Ha, ha…real funny. Listen, what are you doing this Saturday?…no, you do not have a date with Paul Newman…but you are quite free to live with your delusions once you've helped me with this project…here's what I need you to do…"

By the time Calvin returned to the house, Verleen was off the phone and sitting at the kitchen table reading the mail and feeling quite pleased with herself.

On Saturday, Calvin and Old John headed for the barn right after lunch to work on some odd jobs Verleen requested to be done. The blade on the push plow needed to be tightened, the garden hoes all required sharpening, and the gate going into the lean-to on the side of the barn was hanging crooked and getting hard to open and close. There were various vegetable crates and baskets that needed to be sorted, repaired, and stacked in the corner until next spring. After working for an hour or so, Old John announced it was break time. "I sure could use a glass of Miz Vee's sweet tea. Let's head to the house."

Strolling through the back yard, the elderly gentleman seemed to be in an unusually good mood, whistling a tune, and loudly singing snatches of "Old Dan Tucker". Reaching the back porch, he held the screen door open for Calvin.

"SURPRISE!" the small crowd in the kitchen yelled and Calvin stopped in his tracks taking in the scene. Verleen, Gracie, Henry, and a few other of Gracie's grandchildren wore party hats and stood by the kitchen table that held a birthday cake with five lit candles. The kids blew noisemakers, and Calvin could barely make out what everyone was saying. He just stood looking about until Henry grabbed him by the hand and pulled him to the table.

"Blow out your candles, Calvin, so you can open your presents!"

Calvin looked around at Verleen who nodded at him and said, "Make a wish and blow as hard as you can!"

Everyone applauded and shouted, "Happy birthday!" when he blew out the candles.

Unwrapping gifts came next and Calvin didn't seem to know what to do; apparently his birthday party experiences up until today were nonexistent. Henry coached him through each gift and told each giver in turn, "Calvin says, 'thank you'."

The cake, decorated with colorful icing, was served and everyone gathered around the table for a slice with ice cream. Gracie glanced at Old John who was by now also wearing a party hat and was sitting with one of the toddlers on his lap. She nudged Verleen and tilted her head in Old John's direction, "Reckon he's ever had a birthday party of his own? This one's a big hit so maybe we need to plan one for him before long."

"Gracie, that's a wonderful idea."

Once the cake had been consumed, the whole group trooped out to the back yard. Old John set up the Slip 'N Slide, a gift from Gracie, and positioned various sprinklers around the yard to create a water park of sorts. While the kids ran around the yard squealing and laughing and having the time of their lives, Old John manned the water hoses and kept the yellow plastic wet to provide for the best sliding conditions. Gracie and Verleen seated themselves in the porch rockers and watched the enjoyable mayhem that ensued.

"So, Calvin is five years old today," remarked Gracie

"Yep, I decided that today would be his birthday."

"He didn't seem to know how to unwrap a gift. Guess they didn't have birthday parties at the commune," Gracie said dryly.

"Thanks for helping me with the party by providing the cake and some presents, and for bringing a pile of grandkids to make it fun for

Calvin. There's no way I could have baked and decorated that cake in secret. I owe you a big one."

"Oh, you owe me more than one…more like one hundred or so…but who's counting?" Gracie quipped.

"Sounds like you're counting so you can keep me in your debt forever."

"Of course…I'm going to remind you of it every chance I get," Gracie remarked gleefully.

"You vile hussy."

"Vile hussy? That's the best you got, Verleen?"

"Oh, I've got a full arsenal of names for you, but there are children present," Verleen shot back.

"I love you, Verleen," Gracie said with a straight face.

"I love you, too," Verleen replied without hesitation and then added "vile hussy" disguised in a cough.

The two friends broke into laughter that lasted for several minutes. When they finally caught their breaths, Gracie spoke, "Well, I think Old John did pretty good himself keeping Calvin busy 'til we had everything in place."

Looking out at the youngsters, Verleen remarked, "I'm not sure who's having the most fun at this party…him or the kids."

The old gentleman was now squirting each kid in turn with the water hose as they ran by squawking joyfully and his laughter could be heard wafting across the yard.

"Watch this, Nana Vee," Henry called as he got a running start toward the Slip 'N Slide. He belly flopped onto the wet plastic and his speed was impressive right up until the moment he hit the end and the grass caused him to cut a flip. "Ouch!" he yelled as he sat up and grabbed his knee. "I think it's bweeding!"

"I've got this one, Gracie," said Verleen as she headed down the steps. "Come on, Henry, let's go take a look." Taking the little boy by the hand, she headed into the house. "You have a real knack for skinning your knee. We may just have to cut the whole leg off."

"Hey, Calvin, I'll be back in a minute! Nana Vee is going to cut my leg off!" Henry yelled over his shoulder, not the least bit perturbed at the idea of losing his leg.

Verleen set him up on the bathroom counter wiping the mud and grass from his knee. "It's not as bad as we thought…just a little scrape that doesn't even need a Band-Aid. Of course, if it's really bothering you, I can go get the butcher knife," she said helpfully.

"Nawww…it's alright," replied Henry calmly and he grinned up at Verleen.

"Henry, let me ask you something…Calvin talks to you all the time doesn't he?"

"Uh, huh," Henry nodded in affirmation.

"Why is it that you can always hear him but I only hear him sometimes?"

Henry shrugged and scrunched up his face in deep thought. "Maybe you're just not paying attention. You just have to listen right here," and he leaned forward and touched her in the middle of her forehead.

Chapter 33

When the party wound down, Gracie bundled her dripping, wet grandchildren in towels and loaded them into her car and started home. Old John declared that he was worn out from all the excitement, so taking some leftover birthday cake, he headed back down the path to his place.

While Verleen washed up the party dishes, Calvin sat at the kitchen table examining his gifts. There was a Rock 'Em Sock'Em Robot game from Henry, matchbox cars, a yoyo, and a Nerf football from the other kids, and a small rectangular wooden box with a handle filled with small tools from Old John. His gift from Verleen had his attention at the moment. It was a copy of *Bury My Heart at Wounded Knee* and she could hear him turning the pages of the book. He had shown a real interest in reading books about history lately and she thought she would read it, also. It was past time to delve into her Native American background that she knew so little about.

Deciding that this would be a good time to try a little experiment, she sent out some deliberate thoughts in Calvin's direction. *What did you think of your party?*

A silent answer came back quickly. *It was fun. I never had a birthday party before.*

You used your manners and thanked everybody...I'm really proud of you, Calvin.

There was no response and she could tell he was still exploring his new book. So she tried again.

Have you always talked to Henry the way you're talking to me now?

Yes, kids can hear me right away, but grownups can't.

But I hear you.

You didn't at first but then you started to... I think it's because of your sensing.

Can you hear what I'm thinking all the time...or just when I'm trying...like now?

Sometimes your thinking...sneaks out...I try not to hear that but...

Verleen sighed out loud. *Then I guess the surprise party wasn't really a surprise after all.*

It was, Nana Vee. I didn't know what a birthday was so I didn't understand.

For the next several minutes, she washed the dishes and stared out the kitchen window deep in thought and then something dawned on her.

All those times I heard your voice...I was really hearing it in my head the whole time?

Yes.

Verleen took several minutes to deal with that realization.

Do you talk to Boone and Rabbit, too?

Uh, huh, but that's different than talking to people.

What about the chickens and Bessie?

Sure...they like it when I talk to them.

Calvin, can you tell me where you came from and how you got here?

She could feel his indifferent shrug. *No...but this is where I'm supposed to be.*

From then on Verleen was more conscious of their ability to converse with just thoughts and she deliberately projected her thoughts from time to time instead of accidentally like before.

September flew by and the pumpkin patch flourished. The days and nights grew much cooler and fans around the house were no longer needed most of the time. This was Verleen's favorite season and she thrived on the cool fronts that moved in from the north bringing a different smell and feel to the air. Old John cut some plywood for signs that would advertise the pumpkin patch and Verleen and Calvin worked on getting them painted.

"That looks right nice, boy," Old John said when surveying their handiwork.

"I think that's gonna bring in the customers we are hoping for," Verleen agreed. "Mistah John, I'm afraid supper's gonna be late today. I have a few errands this evening. Come around right before dark and it will be ready."

Old John nodded his understanding. Returning his tools to the shed, he waved goodbye at the edge of the yard before setting out on the path through the woods. Verleen looked down at Calvin and winked and the little boy winked back.

When the old gentleman emerged from the woods at the appointed time, he was surprised to see several people sitting around a fire in Verleen's back yard. He hesitated for several moments and then Calvin ran across the yard and grabbed him by the hand, tugging him toward the fire.

"I don't mean to intrude on your company, Miz Vee," the old man said softly.

Verleen snorted. "Nonsense! These folks are here for you. Gracie and I decided it was about time for you to have a birthday party also!"

Old John looked around at Gracie, Earl, and little Henry sitting about the small fire and then he looked down at Calvin. "Did you know 'bout this?" he asked the little boy.

Calvin nodded enthusiastically.

"But Miz Vee, you don't know when my birthday is," he protested.

"I decided it was in October so…happy birthday! And I also decided it was the perfect time for a wienie roast."

"Then I just has one more question…will there be cake and ice cream?" he asked.

"You better believe it!" Verleen laughed and with that the party was underway.

Gifts were presented and unwrapped with Calvin and Henry helping. From Gracie and Earl, Old John received a pocket knife with a wood inlay handle engraved with his name and a fancy pocket watch and chain from Verleen. Calvin's gift was a new felt hat that Old John put on right away and wore for the rest of the night.

"Calvin picked it out and insisted on paying for it out of his piggy bank," Verleen said proudly.

Henry had given Old John a box of six monogrammed handkerchiefs which were going to come in handy since the one the old man had pulled out of his pocket was growing damp from all the eye wiping he was doing.

Wienies and hot dog fixings waited along with roasting sticks on a table set up on the porch. Cake and ice cream and the singing of "Happy Birthday" followed the hot dogs and everyone sat back rubbing their full bellies, laughing and telling stories that always seem to arise when sitting around a fire. When there was a lull in the conversation, Gracie pulled out pictures of Cathy's newborn and proudly showed off the newest addition to the Sheppard dynasty. Then she announced Earl's upcoming retirement and related their plans to take a trip to the East Coast to see some of the sights there.

"When you get back, we'll have another party for Earl's retirement," Verleen remarked.

"And after that, what are we going to celebrate next?" Gracie asked.

"Well...there's Thanksgiving in November, Christmas in December and we can always throw in Hanukkah for good measure...I'm pretty sure I can think of another reason for a party come January."

"You've turned into a regular socialvert, Verleen."

"A what?"

"A socialvert, someone who is outgoing and grogogerious."

"Earl, what is she talking about?"

"I have no idea. Most of the time I can't make out what she's saying...but that's okay. I didn't marry her for her brain. Her pappy promised me I'd inherit lots of oil wells, so naturally when she begged me to marry her, I said 'yes'---"

"Earl Sheppard, you're lying like a dog. You better thank your lucky stars that I agreed to that first date or you'd be living in misery today with Blanch Comeaux."

"What in the world does Blanch Comeaux have to do with anything?"

The teasing argument between the couple went on for some time with Verleen interjecting remarks to keep it going and everyone laughed at the ridiculousness of it all. Old John came out of his shell and talked more than usual and Verleen was beginning to think he was showing signs of becoming a "socialvert" too.

The wonderful evening ended late with no one really wanting to break up the party. Finally, Earl and Gracie told Old John "happy birthday" one last time and steered the yawning Henry to their vehicle. While Verleen took the leftover food into the house, Calvin and Old John put away the chairs and doused the fire which had burned down to coals. Then Calvin walked Old John to the edge of the yard and hugged the old man goodbye and Verleen waved from the porch and called, "Goodnight, Mistah John!"

"I had the time of my life, Miz Vee. Y'all sure know how to party." The full moon lit the way down the familiar path and they could hear him whistling and humming as he headed home.

CALVIN! The boy jerked upright in bed and looked about. Something had pulled him from a deep sleep. The glow of the moon poured through the bedroom window and he could see nothing that was out of the ordinary. Then it hit him like a ton of bricks. He threw back the covers and raced from his bed and across the hall to Nana Vee's room. Climbing onto her bed, he saw that she looked to be peacefully asleep except that she was too still and quiet. Laying both of his hands on her chest, he failed to detect the rise and fall of breathing and there was no heartbeat. He closed his eyes and willed all his energy down his arms and into his hands causing them to begin to warm and glow in the dim room and he concentrated with all his might, just as he had done before…on the night of July 4th.

He removed his hands but she remained still and lifeless. He placed his hands on her chest and directed his energy again with such force that sweat began to run down his forehead. When he removed them, he waited for her to draw a breath and stir but she did not. He took a deep breath, centered his entire being and gathered all the force within his power. His hands were already glowing when he laid them on her chest and he pushed his energy into her, dangerously giving more than he should of his own life force. He held them there for several minutes, his eyes scrunched tightly closed in effort. Pulling his hands away slowly, he looked down on her face and realized that this time it was not going to work.

Laying his head down on her chest he began to sob uncontrollably and it was sometime later when he finally returned to his own room. He found his green, knitted cap, pulled it on, and returned to the open doorway of Verleen's room pausing long enough to whisper in the dark.

I love you, Nana Vee. I will always remember what you taught me.

Taking nothing else with him, the boy called Calvin walked through the kitchen and out the back door. The low-hanging moon glowed off the tops of the orange pumpkins that peeked through the large leaves on the vines as Calvin skirted the patch followed by Boone and Rabbit.

Reaching the edge of the yard, he turned and patted each animal on the head giving them mental instructions as he did. Looking back at the dark, still house one more time, he drew a ragged breath, turned, and set off walking through the tall grass and into the woods. Under the full moon, the big trees cast dark shadows that quickly swallowed him and when Boone could see him no longer, he began to bay with a mournful wail that echoed through the forest. An owl in a nearby tree took up the lament and when Boone hushed, the hoot owl's call was long and lonesome in the silent trees.

Epilogue

A few days later

The tall, slim, young man strolled down the path of the public gardens pausing now and then to smell the intoxicating scents of the flowers wafting on the gentle breeze. He moved gracefully in his lightweight robe and nodded politely in greeting to others who were out and about enjoying the evening air.

Reaching a park bench, he sat and exhaled a sigh of relief. As he leaned back and gave himself over to the pleasant ambiance of the afternoon, the older gentleman who already inhabited the bench spoke quietly.

"Good afternoon…enjoying the gardens?"

The young man glanced over at the man. "Immensely…the flowers are especially fragrant…more so than I remember."

The older man nodded. "I'm sure it seems that way since you've been away so long." There was a pause before he spoke again. "I'm glad to see you are looking so well. We were beginning to worry."

The young man replied, "I apologize for my lateness. I was unavoidably detained."

"I'm sure by now you know that the final decision has been made, so I was surprised to receive your request for this meeting," the older man said seriously.

"I am well aware."

They both fell silent as families and couples strolled past the park bench.

When they were once more alone, the older man spoke first, "The others have all returned and their reports concur. Their findings have been examined and scrutinized thoroughly."

The young man looked off across the landscape and did not reply.

"So why are we here? Why did you ask to see me?" the older man asked impatiently.

The young man chose his words carefully. "I fear what is to come and I am of the opinion that we should postpone undertaking any action."

The older man looked at him sharply and studied the young man's face. "Years of evidence have led us to this determination and we **do** understand the upheaval and chaos that will take place once the plan is executed. We did not make this decision in haste. It has taken us decades to reach this conclusion." His voice carried the gravity of his words.

The young man ran his hand through his hair in frustration and looked off through the purple glow of the evening light.

The older man asked, "Did you not witness for yourself the evidence the others reported?"

"Yes," the young man answered reluctantly.

"Crime and violence?"

"Yes."

"Pollution?"

"Yes."

"Greed?"

"Yes."

"Corruption?"

"Yes."

"War?"

"Yes," his voice getting softer with each answer.

"Then you know what will happen if they continue on this path and the end result will be devastating for every living being. The delicate balance of our world…and all worlds…will be forever altered. We can't afford that…so the time has come for us to intervene and that means taking control."

"But, respectfully, Chancellor, once the wheels are set in motion, there will be no going back. I am strongly convinced the council should delay its plans for now and allow these humans more time."

It was the chancellor's turn to be frustrated.

"Young man, what do you know that we don't? What does this species have as their best hope…other than us? What on their world is powerful enough to alter their course? Just give me something…anything to take back to the council."

The young man with the deep brown eyes looked up at the twin, violet moons high in the twilight sky and took a deep breath before answering.

"Prime Chancellor, have you ever heard of a nana?"

Author's Notes

While Berryville and Lolly Springs are fictional towns in Southeast Texas, they are loosely based on real towns that exist. Other landmarks mentioned, such as the Neches River and the Big Thicket are real places. The National Park Service established the Big Thicket National Preserve in 1974, and today it covers over 113,000 acres which is smaller than its original size, having been diminished by logging companies and the encroachment of human habitation. It's a diverse ecosystem that contains swamps and forests as well as a variety of wild animals.

In 1974, the United States Congress enacted the first major federal legislation addressing child abuse and neglect. Before that time, many displaced children fell through the cracks, and sadly that still happens today despite the laws and policies in place. Until 1975, handicapped and disabled children were not required to attend public school since there were no educational programs designed to meet their needs.

Acknowledgments

Much appreciation goes to Sheila Keeler who reads my manuscript before publishing, looks for holes in the plot, and gives me advice on character development with a wonderful objectiveness that every writer values. Bless your heart! (as we say in the South) You're a real trooper to wade through a raw manuscript and to answer my endless questions, all the while relieving my insecurities as a writer.

Without a doubt, Amber Mansfield and Carrie Beth Forse served as inspiration for Gracie. Their ability to invent words and twist common idioms and southern sayings into a mangled mess is a unique talent they both posses, and they provide as much comic relief in real life as Gracie does in the story. Thanks for the laughter, you crazy gals!

To my dear friend, Marie Todd, who supports my writing efforts by being my editor and sounding board, I am truly grateful for our close friendship which is exactly like Verleen and Gracie's and is one that has endured for many years. Here's to many more years of lengthy conversations and shared secrets!